D0982521

ADAMS FALL

Adams Fall

Sean Desmond

THOMAS DUNNE BOOKS
ST. MARTIN'S PRESS
NEW YORK

THOMAS DUNNE BOOKS
An imprint of St. Martin's Press

www.stmartins.com

Design by Nancy Resnick

Library of Congress Cataloging-in-Publication Data

Desmond, Sean, date
Adams fall / Sean Desmond.—1st ed.
p. cm.
ISBN 0-312-26254-X
1. College students—Fiction. 2. Cambridge (Mass.)—Fiction. I. Title.

PS3554.E842 A64 2000
813'.6—dc21

00-034497

First Edition: October 2000

10 9 8 7 6 5 4 3 2 1

For SMC

Think of it:
The very place puts toys of desperation,
Without more motive, into every brain
That looks so many fathoms to the sea
And hears it roar beneath.

—*Hamlet*, I. iv

Adams Fall

I remember the year began strangely.

I had recently finished moving back into Adams House when there was a blackout through the entire Boston area. That night I went up to the roof and sat on the ledge overlooking the reticent, dark city. The summer was dying down to a breeze. I could make out the shadows of the city's skyline, but as night settled in and fewer cars lighted the streets, the darkness grew and grew. I can picture that darkness from the room I am in now. In the darkness I sleep and feed.

It was my senior year of college. A year that was supposed to be full of new experiences—the beginning of the rest of my life. This was what those years of hard work and study were for. This was when it all paid off and something right before graduation showed you the light. But instead

I got caught under some fateful wheel and my life became a repeat of tired history.

On the night of the blackout the headaches started. They weren't sharp migraines, but a dull, constant pressure that muddled my memory of simple details. I had trouble concentrating and looking past the face value of any given day. Many people said I was sick, and I can understand that. My roommate, Billy, was sick. He committed suicide. But he was also right—whether he knew it or not.

As I sat there on the rooftop and gazed over the thousands of silent buildings huddled in the darkness, I was beginning to see things in a new way. It takes so much anger in a person to see this way. It's a kind of vision that cannot be blinded or diminished—it seems clearer in the dark, but is undisturbed by the light. Everything that night was heightened in its nervousness—as if the city were afraid and waiting cautiously for the sun. Maybe the automatic coffeemaker and alarm clock radio wouldn't come on, but the sun would soon shine and smile. The light of day helps us do this, that, and the next thing. In the light of day we begin again; that's when we fix and resolve. I can't see the sun rise now but I can tell from activity in the hall when it's daytime. I can hear the ignorant confidence in their steps. Tasks being set out and finished as if life were nothing more than a checklist. All this progress and order because of the sun.

That semester, some memory mingled with the present, I won't deny that. Caught in some demented form of déjà vu, I was ready to break forward, and that house, that whole damn school, kept me waltzing in the past. What I can't seem to reconcile is the hold over events he had, and the continual fog I was walking around in. It was like going to a party, having a few beers, and cresting on that first wave of mild drunkenness. The kind of drunk where you're more than happy to hear yourself talk. The kind of drunk when you're so witty and thoughtful that you must have everyone's ear. Then you go to the bathroom and catch yourself in the mirror. Staring into the reflection, you have no idea who that person really is. You don't even recognize yourself on the outside, never mind all the motives and thoughtless reasons that lurk behind the eyes. How does that person in the mirror make any sense, let alone function? The thought, the reflection, is not even sobering. It just drifts vaguely on until you finally come to terms with this: yeah, you're fooling no one, except maybe yourself.

There was a moment that semester which speaks to everything that happened. It was a few months after the blackout. Maeve had come into and out of my life and I was up on the roof again in a foolish, maudlin vigil for her. You can't begin to understand how tired I was at this point. I had been up on that roof every night for over two weeks—that's how I know what happened. I was patient and waited. And on the night in question as they say, he shows up on the roof. Not Billy, but my dark angel. I can't tell you much about him now. You wouldn't believe me. It takes a little time and circumstance to explain the situation.

At any rate, the two of us get to chatting. I was very angry about what had happened to Maeve. He preyed on this, which confounded me further. The longer we talked, the less it all explained.

That's until I realized my own astonishing self. In the midst of obligations, I had lost a sense of purpose. I was too busy impressing others. I had forgotten for whom all the schooling was intended. In order to face him, I had to know myself. You must understand that all these problems begin inside a person. They can grow there for years and years in the darkness of a chided, unused heart. And the College, with its cruel history, had much to do with this blossoming of sorts. Once I realized what I was, then I understood him. You could even say this is his story and I've corrupted it.

And all the blood spilt for it. For what? The truth? An answer? No, just me. Just me and the useless report of what happened.

Of this, I am certain as the sunrise and in no need of your help. When night comes, I go to my bed like a grave.

This story began a couple of weeks before Halloween. I came down to the dining hall to find Rosie on a Monday morning and there were the results of the first wave of midterms on page one of the College paper. Karen Henry, Sidwell Friends, College class of '95, and daughter of Senator Albert Henry, had thrown herself off Weeks Bridge into the near-frozen Charles River. She was found downstream near the Boston University boathouse. A women's crew coach saw her first and dragged the body into her scull. Friends hadn't seen Karen over the past few days and had assumed she was cramming for midterms.

"That makes three from our class and four this year," Rosie sniffed and opened her notebook.

I sat down. Rosie didn't say hello. Her friends Susan

and Happy were sitting across from me. Susan toyed with the last bits of flotsam in her cereal. Happy breezed through the crossword, only announcing the clues she knew the answers to immediately. I admit I never liked either of them. What does it matter at this point? To me, they embodied the irritating self-absorbed qualities I chose to ignore in Rosie. On a good day, they were simply argumentative. On a bad day, they were harpies with a deluded sense of entitlement. I put up with them because they posed no real threat and I didn't need to put added pressure on my relationship with Rosie.

None of us at the table that morning was terribly upset. None of us knew the senator's daughter that well. We were a little jaded by suicide, you could say. In fact, suicide was how I ended up Rosie's boyfriend. We had known each other for some time before we started going out. That's because Rosie was dating my freshman roommate, Billy. Billy was a normal guy by the College's warped standards—smart, driven all his life to be on top, and studying economics to keep his piles of money straight later in life. Billy was a fine roommate; he was neat, easy to talk to, never loud nor very drunk.

Billy hanged himself from the shower curtain rod April of our freshman year. Rosie and I had been sleeping together for about a month prior to Billy's suicide. It's not easy to explain how that started. We shared a history requirement second semester and we'd meet in the library reading room to study together. Rosie really did love Billy then. So I don't know. I badly wanted to be with someone, and she knew it. But she didn't use me either. You really can't judge someone by the mistakes they make that first year of college. You're not even a real person then, you're more a glob of adolescence pinned on its own awkwardness.

Up to the day he committed suicide, we were certain Billy didn't have the faintest idea of what was going on. But then they found the note he left, which quoted an obscure biblical passage about sinners and fools. It also went through the normal laundry list of problems—pressures to succeed, overwhelmed with work, exams looming—but that Bible verse and a constant restating that he was seeing things "clearly for what they were" hit close to home. Billy killed himself on a Saturday night. Timing things, it seemed, so Rosie would find him first.

His words in the suicide note were both pitifully melodramatic and venomously specific. The strange thing was that he didn't seem to blame himself. What I remember about him the days before was happy and pain-free. I guess he had made his mind up on the subject and felt the relief of knowing what he was going to do. It was as if he knew himself to be healthy and thought everyone else was sick. It all went to prove that people at that school could be screwing you over and guessing such was as sure as knowing so. Rosie was sent home that semester and given straight A's. I was moved out of the room and given a prescription for Prozac.

In a weird way, Billy's suicide brought Rosie and me closer together. We were the only two people who may have known the motive for his suicide, and that secret bound us together. We waited for a year after Billy's death before going out in public together. Nonetheless, rumors were floating around and I could tell people talked about us. Walking through the dining hall I caught looks and brows that had the gears of suspicion raising them. Billy's death was long forgotten, but people still cast aspersions on us. What Billy might or might not have known became overshadowed by what others inferred.

So the death of Karen Henry was not going to stir what all of us at that table had tried to bury for three years. The rest was chalked up to being of a certain status and social profile. Karen Henry was probably a social bee stung by the vituperations of her fellow wasps. It was a cold, aloof calculation, but what emotional investment is expected for silver spoons and Barbie dolls? How hard could that life be, and how much sympathy could we have for such tragedy?

"So was her boyfriend sleeping around on her?" I asked, turning the page. Rosie paused ever so slightly, but did not look up at me.

"She was in my section for conflict resolution," Happy said. "Let's just say she wasn't the sharpest knife in the drawer."

Happy wanted to be an entertainment lawyer. She was still pissed that someone had stolen all her thesis notes from her room the first week of the semester. She had spent the whole summer attending some trial of a serial killer in Oregon and without her notes was back to square one. I wasn't surprised it had happened. Happy was a misnomer. Rosie, Susan, and I were what was left of her so-called friends. Count the ex-boyfriends, the people she shouted at drunk while at parties, and then the miserable folk who shared tutorials with her and you had a pretty long list of suspects.

We were all seniors at the College, which was the source, channel, and delta of our endless social critique. As one might expect, we'd spent our whole lives kissing ass to get there and a lot of overachieving neuroses had built up along the way. I remember coming home from third grade with a test I got a ninety-five on, and my father, first thing, asked me what happened to the other five points. That sort of thing instilled success, but with a sharkish attitude I clearly recognized in all of my fellow classmates.

And by the time you're a senior at the College you've met everyone better and smarter than you. Then it's all about discovering the chinks in each other's armor. That is how you can come to the opinion that your average College class of sixteen hundred students is not the smartest sixteen hundred adolescents on earth, but the sixteen hundred sycophants and psychopaths who best knew how to fill out the application. Among the snobs and the nerds, the field of competition was strewn with selfishness and bullshit. The result was a disgusting, incendiary admixture of achievement and insecurity.

I lived in Adams House, B-entry. It's the stone monster that hulks over the junction of Bow and Arrow Streets. A and B entries, also known as Westmorely Court, were built around the turn of the last century. Some years ago, the dean of the College was so fed up with his upperclassmen that he kicked them out of the Yard into houses down by the Charles. Westmorely Court was one of the posher places to dwell and eventually became part of the Gold Coast—a series of snooty residences and final clubs running along Mount Auburn Street.

Adams is the closest house to the Yard and farthest from the Charles. Unlike the Georgian red bricks which make up ninety percent of the campus, Adams runs a gamut of eccentric architectural styles. B-entry in particular has a severe, Gothic quality to it. The floors are checkered with black and white marble tiles that recede into shadowy asymptotes which don't quite seem to reach their vanishing point. The walls are oak-paneled and have been stained into black. The dark strength of the hall is completed by a huge wrought-iron banister and slab stairway that rises to capacious landings on each of the three upper floors. Despite the size of the hallways, the combined wattage of the fluorescent lights throughout the entry is less than that of a reading lamp.

Franklin Roosevelt lived in B-16, the last room on the left, first floor. His room is fairly commonplace aside from the bright, high ceilings and ornate carvings in the oaken mantelpiece. The bathroom from his day is still intact—an old-fashioned toilet with the overhead box and rope plunger and a giant porcelain lion's-paw tub with a small stepladder rising to its lip. People will tell you that he had the special bathroom for his polio, but Roosevelt didn't come down with the disease until twenty years after college.

Across the hall and halfway down from his room is the door to the Adams House pool. The decor and detailing of the pool room seem ancient and heavy, like a miniature version of the Baths of Caracalla. The pool is completely indoors and its tiled bottom is a wild mosaic of zoomorphs and floral curlicues.

For decades Adams House was costly to live in and therefore all the more exclusive and conservative. After World War II, housing costs were reined in for scholarship kids and young men on the GI Bill, and Adams, while desperately clinging to its haughtiness and tradition, became more and more the arts house on campus. Black turtlenecks replaced dinner jackets in the dining hall. The pool was closed after too many bacchanals, or so the freshmen are told before they move down from the Yard. Adams still attracts the hipster set, but these days that equals a bunch of suburban kids reveling in sexual ambiguity. The range of habits and activities is narrow and annoying—discussion of the "other," which rapper has the most cred, which TV shows would Friedan and de Beauvoir watch, where's the subculture, why no movements, deconstructing X, and when all else fails, pledge allegiance to something ironic and low-fi.

I lived on the fourth floor, B-46, in a fairly spacious single. There were few singles available in the house and I considered myself lucky. The front door to B-46 opens onto a short hallway with the bathroom and shower to the left, the closet straight ahead, and the main room to the right. The ceilings are about fifteen feet high. The main room is a simple square—the bed in one corner, and the desk by a pleasant set of French doors that open onto a small balcony which was perfect for smoking. A dresser, bookshelves, and noisy radiator take up the rest of the space.

It was a haul up all those stairs, but the fourth floor was more quiet and secluded than the rest of the house. And that's exactly why I took it. I was an English major with a thesis to write. My thesis was on Shakespeare, his problem plays, and the development of his middle style. It sounds like crap, but *Troilus and Cressida, Measure for Measure,* and *Hamlet* were in vogue with the department and my adviser. I admit, it was a bit of a cop-out—a thesis on Shakespeare—but I knew my way around the plays and I had much to do senior year in addition to my thesis.

Rosie, my girlfriend, lived on the second floor of B-entry in a triple with Susan and Happy. Rosie was a good, honest girl, and despite all our latter-day problems, I truly loved her. She was your typical Irish lass—fair skin, dark brown hair, and clear blue eyes. We got along well for a long time, and the simple why analysis would be that we were opposites. She was a realist and I was a failing romantic. She was an economics major ready for the business world. I loathed responsibility if it didn't match my criteria for classic ennoblement. She was conversational, outgoing, and aggressive. I tried to feign mystery and intelligence with withdrawal and moodiness. But we were attracted to each other in this way—we added virtue for knowing the faults of the other. College was an academic trial and emotionally draining for us both and we relied heavily on each other. I cared for her deeply.

But senior year was exhausting, and the cracks began to show. Despite three years of a relationship, we had little in common and she became too serious for my tastes. We fought more and more, but neither of us discussed breaking it off. I was the one who started it; I was the one losing a grip on the relationship. She was so smart and attractive and I admit to being nervous and a headcase. She had changed utterly and so had I. But I knew her before things got to be a mess and she was different. Trying to figure out college was a lot easier with Rosie around, but somewhere along the line I didn't need her help anymore. Nonetheless I couldn't end it or free myself up somehow. It was my first long-term relationship—I had met her family, she wore my ring, that sort of commitment.

So we were drifting apart. Billy was always a tacit reason. He brought us together, but was also a curse on the whole thing, I guess. It's hard now to remember how I loved her, and the beginning of senior year was a busy time made for selfishness and fights with your girlfriend. I was beavering away at a Marshall application for two years of grad school abroad, and Rosie was going through recruitment and consulting interviews. What little time we had was sexless and I'd rather drink tequila and play pinball in the laundry room than listen to her girlfriends squawk and gossip. Either our world was changing or my ideas about what was important were. Call it immaturity like she did. I was too tired at that point to care.

There was something about B-entry that added to this. I loved the seclusion of my room, but the starkness of the hallways and landings left me cold and uncomfortable. Someone stepping on the stairs or closing a door echoed widely. Tricks on the ear were common, and as soon as you were sure someone was outside your room, a door down the hall or on the floor below would slam shut.

All of the entryways in Adams House feed into a system of tunnels that link below the dining hall and main entrance to the house. With a carton of cigarettes you could spend weeks inside Adams, eating, sleeping, and studying without ever going outside. These tunnels are poorly lit, and passing people in them made me bristle. The whole layout and lighting of the house was dismal and added to my reclusiveness. Half the people I didn't know, the other half just gave me that look. So I talked very little to other people, and that suited me fine. In the dim tunnels and stairwells of Adams, my vision became more and more perceptive to shadow play. Alone in my room at night I could keep a careful tally of every door opening and every step into the hallway. My ear for the stairwell became extremely acute. By the end of the semester, each faint sound crawled out of the white noise and echoed endlessly in my mind and sleep. By the end, it was a deafening, pointless affair.

I got up from the table and walked out of the dining hall and Adams House. I turned up Plympton Street, crossed Massachusetts Avenue, and entered the Yard. Within a few minutes, I had Rosie's cool reception at the breakfast table behind me. It was early October but the chill air ran right through me. The oaks and maples in the Yard were nearing their full autumn coloring. The morning was a light gray—the same pale skies that had hovered over the Boston area for the past two weeks. The New England autumn was an ashen limbo I endured impatiently, never quite acclimating to its dreariness.

I passed into the main quad, also known as Tercentenary Theater. To my left was the old Yard, where the administration hall and freshman dorms had stood for centuries. I could even see the top of the dark red gables of Matthews Hall, where I had dormed my freshman year. Karen Henry had also lived in Matthews that year. I only saw her passing a few times in the hallways. There had been too many incidents like hers, and I felt ashamed for not caring.

Matthews was also, of course, where Billy had lived.

Tercentenary Theater is a relatively new part of the Yard, with classroom halls, a library, and Memorial Church to each side of the quad. I trudged past Widener Library and up the steps of Sever Hall for my Monday lecture on Renaissance art. Sever is a thick maroon stone chiseled out by Richardson. It smelled like graduate students and musty wool sweaters. The class was my last College elective, and the historical period tied in nicely to my thesis. The class was taught by Professor Oglesby, a distinguished scholar so old, as the joke went, his lectures went by titles such as "The Northern Renaissance as I Witnessed It" or "When Leonardo and Raphael Sat in Those Same Seats." I took my normal seat in the back of the classroom. From the last row Oglesby was invisible except for a great shock of white hair that bobbed in front of slides of frescoes and canvas close-ups.

Throughout the first few weeks of the semester, I enjoyed Oglesby's slide shows and his lectures. There was an order to the class and to its subject—a steady progression of apprentices on the heels of masters, all on the cusp of change. But as the class approached midterms, I was becoming more and more depressed that this was my last elective. What the hell had I been doing all this time? Chasing academic carrots, I suppose. After class that day I had to take lunch back to my room and work on my Marshall application. Then I had to head into Boston and finish up my magazine internship. It was my last week at the magazine and I was giving it up to add time to write my thesis. After that, I went to the library to reshelve books and study the rest of the night. A dreary day with no expectations—a day crammed with résumé builders and loan payoffs. I was always cynical, but by senior year I saw nothing but the tedious steps toward a burnt-out career or frustrated life playing Frisbee with other grad students inside a self-preserving bubble called the academy. What wonderfully bleak and disillusioning prospects.

Another reason I was taking this elective was for the student body—I loved fine arts majors. They were ninety percent women and one hundred percent idle rich. I pictured them growing up on the Upper East Side within a stone's throw of Museum Mile. It was laughable how high on themselves these girls were. It was equally ridiculous how dolled up they were for a professor who couldn't see past the first row. Then again they were well put together and did catch the eyes of a few Eurotrash teaching assistants. I tried to arrive early some days just to watch the processional masque as each of them entered the classroom and air-kissed their sisters of the arts. These women didn't talk, they squealed like exotic birds.

As Oglesby gummed on about Cimabue and the seven great ciboriums of Urbino I pictured myself as some sort of kept boy to these future socialites. Daddy would donate the loft and I would spend my afternoons wandering toward some higher purpose. The lucky debutante (let's call her Brittany) would be busy coordinating a new opening—some upcoming graffiti artist arrested on the F train. Then, in the evening, she would hurriedly leave word for me with her cell phone and I would skip along the cobblestones of SoHo to attend her nightly fête. In the summers, lobster dinners at the estate in Easthampton. We'll see if Brittany's mummy is keeping up her figure—playing lots of tennis, darling?—maybe cash that chip in. I'd just behave and tune out the whole family's waspy monotony. Brittany would, of course, be a sex addict. It would be an ideal yet loveless affair. Perhaps even hateful and passionate. But I would know that from the start. Besides, what would I be losing?

I especially lusted after Maeve O'Hara. She had a way about her that beguiled the trust-fund arrogance displayed by the other girls in the class. She was perfectly demure with wet brown eyes. Her figure was a series of correct answers and her legs could most certainly cause problems. From the back of the room, I fixated on her dark brown hair, which was full and gorgeous. Several times a class she would tease her hair up and over the chairback. Then she'd raise it dexterously over the smooth, bare crescent of her neck and pull it through a rubber band or clip. Minutes later, she'd pull it out again, her hair dropping down in a marvelous, always unexpected way. In the words of our beloved professor, she had chiaroscuro which added plenty of mysterioso. She intrigued me greatly.

"The easiest way to know what period of Renaissance art you are in is to study the trees. In this early Piero di Cosimo the trees look more like bushes on popsicle sticks. Botticelli did better—SLIDE—with this forest, but it's all at one distance, on one eye level. SLIDE. Titian painted trees that blow, bend, and rape the canvas. The figures are threatened by their environment, the pastoral is replaced with the tempest, and the force is evocative and darkly romantic. The trees are no longer adornment, but possess sheer will."

The lecture was putting me into a coma, and I cursed myself for forgetting to bring along a cup of coffee. I was tired of all the academic flexing and hamster-wheeling that was going on at that school. Great art made greater by priggish, arrogant academics. Don't get me wrong—I wasn't your average student, and was perhaps more snide than most. But there was something detrimental and creepy to all of this, the whole system of academic back-handing and refinement—it took the brightest people and narrowed their area of study into a specialized nothing. I scanned the room and found most everyone attentive and deep in analysis of the slide. They looked mesmerized, dronelike.

And in the midst of this churning, intellectual machine where was I? Flailing if not drowning. My good grades and papers were overlooked by the English department. I was fed up with the race to know a little more and score a point higher. My last dance was the Marshall application—two years in Stratford studying the Bard. The running was tight and now I don't even know why I bothered. At the time, though, I needed some hope and was looking for an excuse to travel. I wanted to pub-crawl and drink yards of beer. I wanted to be hours from London, Paris, and Amsterdam. I wanted to get out of there.

Maeve tilted her head to study the slide, bringing her hair off its dark groove on her shoulders. She had a smoothness and charm in her motions. Sprezzatura. I looked up at the figures in the Titian. They seemed rubbed out, wispy, mythic. The forest whirled in the storm, the brushstrokes crude and jagged. The effect swept the canvas into some Elysian past I could not fathom. This was a cloistered island in the Adriatic. A world that lay just beyond the horizon, or, in the case of this painting, where the hazy mountains met the sea. But we were here and I glanced down once more at Maeve. She was angelic and brazenly real in the same breath.

"What the trees tell us composes a major current that runs throughout the Renaissance and this class—a question of perfection and introspection. We move from the realm of ideas into the perfection of the human form and finally delve into a world of mannerism where emotional contortion rather than supine figuralism is the ideal projected onto a landscape."

Supine figuralism—I had to write that one down. I liked Oglesby but I wondered how much of his lectures was bullshit. Just when I began to follow his train of thought, I was derailed by skepticism. Did he know so much that it came out as fierce generalization? Or was he trying to talk down to my level and therefore devolved into such themes and epochal geists? How could anyone speak with authority or certainty?

"Mannerism is unusual and appealing in the myths it chooses—mostly Ovid and the tribulations of the Christ Child."

Oglesby had one of those terrific mid-Atlantic accents. I bet as a child he grew up around a lot of adults and learned to talk that way. His throaty lilts were full of a clear respect for certain masters and a self-assured disdain for the lessers. Imagine taking a class where you had to guess by intonation what artists were passé, and which were on the exam.

"What del Sarto fails to see—SLIDE—Bronzino masters in this period."

And with that, the bell in Memorial Church rang in the tenth hour of the day. I knew Maeve in passing from previously shared classes—enough to say hello and jabber about a course's hardships and foibles. I also knew how to time my departure so as to catch her lighting a cigarette outside Sever. That day it worked beautifully and I caught her ducking behind the door to light a match.

"Hey you." She looked at me with a bit of desperation. I fumbled for my Zippo. "What did you think of the lecture?"

"He's quite a character," I said.

"I like Oglesby," she said with a little scorn. "At least he doesn't get mired in details. And the slides go well." Her cigarette was up and smoking, no thanks to me.

"Where are you headed?" I asked.

"Over towards Winthrop." And I took a few steps that way with her. I was about to cut out when she looked me straight.

"Are you going to the Advocate this Friday?" She was very matter-of-fact in her flirting, if this was flirting.

"Are you?" I cringed at the question—Rosie had most likely penciled herself in for dinner and a movie.

"Probably. My roommate is throwing the party."

And with that she smiled and split off on a path across the Yard. Suddenly, the bleak morning light was filled with all the ripeness of autumn. Each step across the Yard added to my ego trip. I'm not good-looking—modest to plain, I would rank myself—but I always wished for (and tried to practice) some sort of allure that a girl might pick up on. I took Maeve's invitation as a swallowed hook on that allure.

Confident for the first time and perhaps the last, I caught a last glimpse of her exquisite, supple legs as she cut around the corner of the library.

That week passed quickly and on Friday I worked the afternoon away in the library reshelving books. Widener, where I shelved, is mammoth—ten floors with nearly fifty miles of books. The exterior has a traditional colonnade and pediment, but inside lurks a dark maze of cast-iron stacks and over three million volumes. The library is a disorganized hive of pulp with twice as many books as fit the shelf space. After three years of roaming and shelving in the stacks, I knew every corner and study carrel. On a long afternoon I would speed through my shelving and hide on one of the lower, subterranean levels, reading with one eye and watching for the stacks supervisor with the other. Sometimes I would just wind through the darkness of the lower levels. The older collections were stored in these areas, and there was something quiet and comforting in the pervasive smell of book rot and binding glue.

Widener is connected by tunnels to two other libraries—Lamont, which is where the undergraduates study, and Houghton, which houses the rare books and the College archive. I had done some work in Houghton but wasn't as familiar with it as with Widener and Lamont. And almost all of my jobs were in the College archive, where I had done book searches and shelf reads. The archive, which is completely underground, was built in the 1970s and has the modern, sterile charm of a hospital—white walls, orange carpets, and an unblinking overkill of fluorescent lighting. It is also where the College has experimented with movable stacks.

Movable stacks are just like normal stacks except there's no space between them. The whole row of stacks is put on runners, and when you want a book, you just push the green button at the appropriate row, and the stacks roll open. Where you have five stacks in a normal library you can put ten using this system. Sensors in the floor pick up your weight when you enter the stacks. They turn on the lights for that particular row and don't allow others to move the rows—that is, the sensors won't allow the rows to be moved and trap a person inside.

Unfortunately the movable shelves were getting older and the sensors in the floor not so reliable. One time I left a step stool inside a row. It weighed enough for the sensors to notice. Nonetheless, the lights went off and the row started to close, ramming the stool through three sections of the books.

That Friday, though, I was hiding on Widener's D-level awaiting the five-o'clock bell. I had been alone for hours down there and out of boredom had traced the complex lattice of pipes running through the guts of the library. I tracked the electrical ducts and plumbing lines, and from the radiators discovered where the steam pipes came and went. Behind and beneath the western wall of that floor lie giant steam tunnels that run from one end of campus to the other. Late that afternoon, the heat was being turned on for the first time.

It began with just the clean sound of water filling the pipes. These rushing and spilling sounds rose for about ten minutes. I stood up from the ladder on which I was sitting and drew closer to the pipes. A strange gurgling grew and grew and then stopped completely. Some tricklings could be heard here and there for several minutes, and then the giant tunnels began to creak. I put my hand to the wall and was surprised to find it cool. The creakings grew into deep moans that echoed through the narrow stacks, airshafts, and carrels. Soon the noise of metal stretching was enormous and encompassing to the point where I was certain the tunnels and wall would break open. Smaller, offshoot pipes clanged up and down, near and far, from where I stood. I took my hand from the wall and found it covered in a film of sweat.

Then I heard someone walking my way and ducked into a corner, fearing it was the stacks supervisor. I listened closely for a stack light to click on but could only hear plaster slowly curling and cracking. After several minutes I realized I had been tricked by the sharp hisses and stretches of the pipes. Breathing in the growing dampness, I put my hand to the wall again and felt the clean hum of the steam rushing past. I must have stood there for half an hour, deep in the belly of that old building.

Something about the vibration seemed very old and intelligent to me. My head drowned in a soup of steam hisses.

Five o'clock finally came and I raced up the eight flights from D-level to leave the stacks, then back down through the sulking marble domes of Widener's lower exit. I felt the weight of the week gradually lifting—my Marshall application just needed some polishing, I would most likely see Maeve at the Advocate, and I had just a few articles to read for my thesis that weekend. I passed out of the Yard through Dexter Gate and across Mass Ave towards Adams. I checked my mail quickly for applications from grad school. None there, I started walking towards the tunnel heading for B-entry, but then remembered I was meeting Rosie at the master's tea.

The master of Adams was an English professor who lived in Apthorp House, a large, three-story Colonial across Plympton Street in the sophomore quad of Adams. Tea was rarely served at these functions and the two hours were an ideal opportunity for the senior class to put half a bag on before Friday night. Although every house had such a tea they served black-and-tans at Adams.

I strolled into Apthorp House and after a quick survey realized Rosie and her roommates were not around yet. I caught Master Donahue in the corner of my eye and he smiled my way. Donahue taught a James seminar I took my junior year and we knew each other fairly well. I made my way to the back of his house, found a pint glass, and began the slow pour of a Guinness from the kitchen keg. I looked through the kitchen doorway, admiring the adjacent sitting room. This room fanned out from a giant Persian rug. The walls were lined with bookshelves and dark oil paintings. Everything surrounding me was handcarved—the kitchen cabinets, the cornices, doorframes, and bookshelves. On one cabinet, a small nymph was carved into the door and gave the impression it was tugging coyly at the doorknob. I couldn't tell whether the nymph was pulling the cabinet open or holding on to the doorknob for fear of falling. While waiting for my Guinness to settle, I watched Donahue gather a few students around a portrait hanging above the fireplace in the sitting room. The subject was an imperious British gentleman, dressed in a long red coat that unfurled over his chair and partially hid his sword. A closer study of the face revealed a long, Ichabod-like frown.

"Burgoyne was left out to dry by his fellow British generals, who were then set on capturing Philadelphia and couldn't care less about him or his beleaguered army roaming up and down the Hudson Valley. After Burgoyne surrendered at Saratoga, Benedict Arnold sent him here, to Cambridge, where all the old Tory mansions, Apthorp included, were being used as jails for the upper-class British sympathizers. Burgoyne was furious that he had lost his army to a bunch of ragtag colonists and was equally upset at being betrayed and abandoned by Mother England." I remember thinking at the time that being beaten by a bunch of upstate New York hicks seemed the worse of the two. But then came the rest of Donahue's story, which didn't make any sense until much later.

"So Burgoyne stayed in Apthorp under house arrest for three years while the war played out. The general probably hated his captors, but after a few failed attempts at getting King George and Parliament to pay the ransom for his freedom, he settled into College life. With a guard always by his side, he was allowed to wander through the

Yard and take a morning stroll down by the Charles. After two lonely winters passed, he sent for his wife back in England."

Donahue suddenly grew grave. This was a well-rehearsed performance. "Sadly, Burgoyne's wife drowned during her passage to Boston. She had raised the ransom from her family, but that too fell to the bottom of the ocean. News of her death broke the general. He became churlish and demented and would bark like a dog at his captors. He'd go days and nights without sleep and eventually confined himself to the darkness of the wine cellar muttering half-crazed commands to his troops and soft coaxing words to his lost wife."

Donahue really had them hanging on his next word.

"Shortly after the decisive American victory at Yorktown, Burgoyne died mysteriously down in that wine cellar. Most think it was self-poisoning. Perhaps he missed his wife too much, but more likely he was too ashamed to return to England, and there was no way to pay off his mounting debt. You must understand that in those days you paid your jailer a heavy boarding fee."

The irony of inflated boarding costs was lost on the audience—apparently none of them saw their College bills. Donahue's eyes grew frightfully large to the point of self-parody as he gestured across the room and into the main hallway. "At any rate, I swear he still lurks here—behind the creak of a door or in an unexplained clink of wine bottles down in the cellar."

Although I had heard the story before, something in me shivered. I took a sip of beer and watched each of the listening students glance nervously across the hall toward the door leading down to the old house's cellar. Then Donahue raised his glass and gave the story its final toast.

"A man famous only for his great losses, Burgoyne's ghost wanders this house trying desperately to make amends or find some way back to success. I'm certain of it."

A stirring rendition. Stirring enough that I raised my glass and toasted the portrait. Swallow, pour, repeat, and I was immersed in debate with my friend Michael, a fellow English major and probably the only person at that damn school who hated academic and social airs as much as I did.

"I read *To Have and Have Not* for Harper's class." Michael was a rapacious reader, and I have to admit that there was a low-grade competition between us. It was annoying, but not awful, and Michael was a good guy to party with. Nonetheless, even with a close friend I had some guard up.

"Good movie," I said. "Screenplay by Faulkner."

"I'm telling you, this book is terrible. I'm not just talking typical bad Hemingway. This book is so poorly plotted. The guy is supposed to be a cove on the coast of Cuba and you don't know where the boat is, or how many people he's picked up or shot off the damn boat. Freshman year we would have explained this away in a paper about the holes in human consciousness, but I'm telling you the writing is just plain bad."

I smiled. "At least the female characters are fully developed and believable."

He waved me off and came back, "Hey, what are you doing tonight?"

By now, I was wonderfully adrift on a stomachful of stout. I studied the eyes of the Burgoyne portrait as they followed me across the sitting room. The crowd was thinning out. Rosie had still not made her appearance, and our evening together was quickly receding from my mind and care. A few butterflies of excitement rose in my stomach at the underlying suggestion of Michael's question.

"I don't know. The Advocate maybe. Can we talk about Maeve O'Hara?"

"I hear she's a bit chilly."

"Winter is coming on."

"What the hell are you talking about? You're a married man." Michael too knew where this was going.

"Let's get out of here."

I smiled. Thank God for Michael. We headed back to his room in B-entry and smoked a bowl. The weekend was well underway and I felt a deep vibe of relaxation coming on. I drifted along on the fuzziness of it while Michael went on about Karen Henry's suicide.

"I heard he was sleeping around on her."

"The ponce, the pimp even," I said in a Snaggletooth impression.

"I wonder why all the great love songs are anti-love songs." Michael rolled his eyes at me and then raised his beer. "Here's to Karen Henry."

I stared through the muted television. "It's so much easier and cleaner to be angry." My throat was dry from hitting the plants. "Sadness, hate, bitterness, envy—they have their own simple, safe reasons."

Michael laughed and picked up the pipe. "I warned you about this shit."

At that moment, what had all the trappings and suits of a warm high began to give me the spins of woe. As usual I had overdone it and was upset with myself. I sat up on the couch and then lay back down. I watched the TV swirl colors across the room. My whole head became untwirling twine.

• • •

And suddenly I fell back into a swathe of dreams and memories. I was lying on the couch in our common room freshman year. We lived on the fourth floor of Matthews—Billy and me. I was half asleep, worn out from pulling an all-nighter for a paper. The heating pipes gurgled off and on, and it must have been early November. I was thinking about getting up and going to dinner, but I was exhausted and the room was so peaceful and dark. I had decided to sleep a little while longer when I heard a key scratch against the lock.

"Hey, narcolept. Get up, get up."

Billy took his key out of the door and dropped his bookbag in the hallway. Rosie scurried through the door behind him and into our shared bedroom. Rosie was so cute back then. She had that naughty Catholic-schoolgirl charm. Gorgeous long, brown hair (what a mistake that was junior year to cut it), and her blue eyes were so sharp and dazzling. Not a stern bone in her body—cunning and determined, yes—but still very sweet. She never liked me as much as Billy, but even back then we were interested in each other. It was astonishing how much she changed, how prudish and provincial she became. She probably wasn't the most popular or prettiest girl in high school, but that hadn't caused any major damage. Rosie was coming into her own in college and she looked damn good. Of course, between the two of them, I felt closer to Billy. We had hit it off so well as roommates. Billy was so outgoing. By the second week of school he seemed to know everybody, and by association I was part of the scene. But people change a great deal that first semester. They also forget their fast friends and settle into what's familiar and expected. We had just survived our first round of midterms, and college really hadn't taken its toll on us yet. There was already some distancing and selfish roommate crap, but Billy and I tried to play that down. It's hard to imagine now, but I was optimistic. Every day seemed promising, new.

"Get up, lazy, it's snowing."

So I rolled off the couch and stumbled to the window. Sure enough, the first real snowfall of the year. Rosie emerged from the bedroom with all our coats and we ran downstairs. Amazing. The snow was really coming down. The last purple hues of twilight were bending over the Yard, and the snowfall was uncommonly beautiful as it dusted over the rooftops and trees and fluttered down through the soft yellow light of the dorms. Within a few minutes it seemed the whole freshman class had gathered outside. I looked over at Rosie, who was smiling, the snowflakes glistening in her hair. A troupe of jocks was tossing around a football. Snowballs were being shuffled together and packed tight. Even the nerds came out of the science library and skitted around in their oversized down coats. You could feel the anticipation growing for the greatest snowball fight ever. Almost magically, Billy produced a bottle of schnapps.

"Cheers, roommate." And he took a swig, passing it to me. I took a relatively weak sip—I was still waking up—and it tasted like cinnamon-flavored jet fuel. I passed the bottle back, swallowing hard.

So we watched our classmates frolicking in the first snow. I felt infinitely hopeful, like a bright and circumspect Henry Adams on the sidelines trying to make sense of the fray. I was wondering who over the coming years I'd cross paths with, befriend, and never know. I turned around to find Billy and take another try at the schnapps, but he had disappeared. Instead I spotted Rosie, mortified and holding a pile of clothes. Then in the corner of my eye, I saw Billy's ghost-white butt come streaking from behind the Matthews porch. An enormous cheer came up as he rushed across the Yard.

"Oh my God." I started cheering him on. Naked except for his sneakers. And boy was Billy sprinting. He looked in great shape and managed to dodge most of the snowball volleys. I couldn't see his face, but with the snow falling hard and him hurtling across the Yard, it was like watching some graceful and athletic angel. He seemed so happy, so eager to be in that spotlight, and so comfortable with himself. I envied that.

A few minutes later I was smoking and watching half the freshman class following Billy's lead. So many naked people, it was like some sort of Bosch painting—heaven or hell I couldn't tell you. Then Billy returned to our perch outside of Matthews draped in a towel he'd swiped from the laundry room of Weld Hall. He was shivering madly and his chest and arms were flushed and goose-bumped. He reclaimed the schnapps from Rosie and took a swig. The jocks playing football couldn't decide whether it was fruity or cool to streak the Yard together. Rosie scampered off, pretending to run away with his clothes. Billy chased her and dragged her down into the snow. She acted upset and then devilishly tried to steal Billy's towel. He in turn attempted to pull her clothes off and force Rosie into streaking. If there hadn't been dozens of naked people running around throwing snow-balls at each other, it would have been quite a scene. But I was watching their goofing around, and I'll never forget how happy they seemed.

From the minute they laid eyes on each other, Rosie and Billy were in love. They were going out by the end of freshman orientation and were acting like a married couple by the second week of school. They both probably had steady relationships all through high school and they just seized on the security of what they knew. And they were both economics majors. I secretly believed that Rosie wanted to glom off Billy's hard work, but that's too snide on my part. Rosie learned quickly how to get good grades, and the two of them definitely worked well together.

I headed back up to the room, the schnapps having sparked a warm glow in me. I picked up my English lit anthology and thumbed over the onionskin pages. I was just tipsy enough for the poetry assignment. Can you imagine me curled up with my books—half drunk on schnapps, half drunk on the idea that I'd learn it all and be something great? How naïve. It sickens me now.

Twenty minutes later, Billy and Rosie came rambling into the room, pegging me with a couple of snowballs. I ducked behind the arm of the couch, but it was too late. The cold water actually woke me up a bit. Billy, still draped in a towel, crossed the common room and plugged in the electric kettle, and in a few minutes we all had hot chocolate with what remained of the schnapps. Rosie and Billy wanted to watch TV, so I took my book into the bedroom and closed the door. Enough fun now. I had to study. I had to work hard. TV makes you forget what you read.

After a half hour or so I was drifting off into Sidney's sonnets when Rosie knocked quietly and then slipped into the bedroom.

"Come back out and sit with Billy and me. We're bored." I don't think I saw Rosie do a lick of work that first semester. She probably crammed the minimum amount required, but studiousness came later in her college career.

"I should finish this and go get dinner. Have the two of you eaten?" I responded.

"I'm not that hungry." Rosie plunked down on the edge of my bed. She had a very coy look on her face. "Why didn't you streak through the Yard tonight with Billy?"

"I don't know, he was off and running before I knew it. Then afterwards, it seemed old hat." She was touching my leg with her thigh. We both pretended not to notice. Then I inquired, "Why didn't you?"

"Nobody asked."

"Billy wanted you to."

"Billy sees plenty of that." And she sat up on the bed giving me this fake doe-eyed look like some sort of stripper.

"Are you drunk?" I had only seen her drink that one hot chocolate, but then again, with Rosie it didn't take much.

"Maybe." She started to giggle and lost her balance, falling forward across my waist. I could smell her hair. Roses and lemons.

"Get up, you lush." I pushed her away but was so turned on. Such a tease. And brilliant in a way—a purposefully bad performance that was hiding something.

She sat up and regained her poise. In an instant, she was no longer interested in me. She hopped off the bed and turned back to give me this very mock-serious face.

"You know, Billy thinks you like boys."

I felt something cold and white flash through me. It was a stunning accusation, but I had to recover. I had to answer that.

"I'm not gay."

"So you don't have a crush on Billy?" She took a step closer to the bed. Her questions were an odd mix of earnest and rude.

"No."

"Do you have a crush on me?"

"You should be quiet. Someone"—I pointed toward the common room—"might hear you."

"I like you. And I think Billy likes you too." I'm not sure even Rosie knew what game she was playing then.

"Thanks, Rosie, you're swell." I was quite annoyed now. Annoyed but still turned on in a strange way.

"Come out into the common room." And with that she kicked open the door. "Let's play I never."

Billy had put on his clothes and was staring at the evening news. He noticed the door swing open and shouted over his shoulder, telling Rosie to leave me alone. I was in a daze at what had just happened. And Billy's response seemed a little stilted. Another bad performance. It was like he had heard everything. It was like he had sent her in to me. No. Rosie was just teasing and then thought she'd hit a deep nerve.

"Come on, let's play." She rummaged around the room, producing a bottle of vodka.

"I hate this game." But when the mood hit him, Billy would take any excuse to drink. I came back into the common room and sat in a chair by the desk. Rosie parked herself next to Billy on the couch and filled three plastic cups half full of vodka.

Rosie started us off. "I never played this game before." We all drank. The vodka tasted awful and was reminiscent of my mother breathing down my neck.

Billy went next. "I never had sex." We all drank again.

"I never french-kissed a girl." Rosie didn't drink.

"I never french-kissed a boy." I looked over at Billy, who was not drinking. And neither was I.

Billy's turn again. "I never ran naked through the Yard." Billy drank and then refilled his cup.

"I never cheated on my significant other." We all drank.

"Why are you drinking?" Billy asked Rosie.

"Prom. Don't worry, sweetie. My turn." Rosie thought hard for a moment, then curled her lips into a very sly smile. "I never had a crush on anyone sitting in this room."

She smiled at Billy and then darted a look over to me while drinking. "Well, are you going to drink?"

I thought she was talking to Billy, but he had already drunk. I was getting tired of her playing me against Billy. If she only knew. Then again maybe she did know. Maybe she'd put Billy up to it. Or vice versa, with that little scene in the bedroom. No, Rosie just wanted Billy to act a little jealous—to be a little worried.

So I gave them something to worry about and took a drink.

Billy looked away at the television, pretending not to notice. I knew immediately I had fucked up. He wasn't ready for this. Oh, what did he care? Maybe I was wrong. Maybe I was being childish. All of a sudden, I was extremely drunk.

"What was that for?" Rosie asked. Then Billy tried to laugh it off. But Rosie didn't get it and wasn't letting it go.

"I just find you both so damn charming."

Rosie blew me a kiss and Billy had this look of total relief. He hadn't told her. He would never tell anyone. What was there to tell? Nothing happened, you idiot. I guess I should have been relieved. But I wasn't. It made me feel so useless. The ultimate third wheel. And there was something smug in Billy's relief. Something arrogant in that he knew he had it all—the girl, the looks, the friendship of so many others. I was so jealous, yet felt nauseous and trapped by my response. We sat silently for an entire, agonizing minute. I should have realized it was freshman year and people didn't know what they wanted yet, or who they wanted to become. I should have let go. But I couldn't. I felt used.

Rosie burst into another fit of laughter. She cut the tension in the room, but what a disaster. I didn't want to play anymore. Billy was staring at me, waiting for some indication of what I was thinking. I didn't want to be a part of this. They both thought they knew what I wanted, but it wasn't true. Then Billy started to laugh. I tried to get out of my chair, but I was too drunk to stand up. They were both laughing at me. I never drink too much. I never had a crush on you.

And I was going to show Billy. Rosie too. Don't laugh at me.

I woke up on Michael's couch and two hours had disappeared. I could hear Michael in the shower. The TV sat there blithering away like an old person who's chased family from the room. I had a fairly serious headache and no food in my stomach. I got up and yelled to Michael that I'd see him at the Advocate in an hour. I pocketed a couple of buds from the table and stumbled up to my room.

I showered and shaved. Despite an inauspicious start, I was determined to make a good night of it. It had been a while since I'd thought about Billy, but I wasn't terribly freaked out by it. I used to dream of him every night and it was difficult to separate real memories from those dreams. They always started off happy, but then spun downward into my own self-loathing. I would never forget Billy, but I'm not sure what I remembered—so much had to be pushed down and forgotten. It wasn't delusional. Rosie did it too. It was a way of surviving.

I looked around my simple room. There was something ultimately sad about the place. I had left the walls bare and they now seemed to hum with the blotchy fluorescent lights of the hallway and bathroom. The windows and French doors were streaked and in need of serious cleaning. Every step across the room brought a chorus of familiar creaks and snaps from the floorboards. In the several steps from my bed to the closet, the first was a low bellowing warp, followed by a series of sharp cracks on the next three boards that ran into the hallway.

The room was reminiscent in some isolating way of my room back home. And the last time I had been home must have been Christmas, ten months ago. Spring break was spent with Rosie and her family. Come summer, Rosie took some consulting internship counting widgets and flanges in the rust belt. I stayed in Cambridge, holing up in a dirt-cheap walk-up off Central Square. For forty hours a week I interned for the grammar columnist at a magazine in Boston. I researched buzzwords and slang on Lexis/Nexis, answered her fan mail as best I could (I had some very creative differences for the use of "that" versus "which"), and on a slow afternoon I would be sent to the main library off Copley Square to find the first use of words like "hyperborean" and "ermine." It was a somewhat lonely stretch in August, but overall the ten months suited me just fine. I was an only child and I just didn't need the grief from my parents. My mother, when not sucking down her second vodka collins, was overbearing and depressed. My father still didn't know why I'd passed up a full scholarship at a state school and put the family in debt well into the twenty-first century. We had the kind of relationship where I told them nothing bad, and they expected nothing good. It wasn't a broken home. We just coped with each other, and nothing ever grew of that. There was no love in our family. Our conversations were matter-of-fact and painful, like a walk in the tides of a cold ocean. Both of my parents were retired, and the small tract house I'd grown up in was too cramped with bad memories for me. And believe me, my family life is not some sort of missing link to my personality. Don't put this information into some half-witted theory. My life before college was a long, lonely wait to leave the suburbs. I had escaped that place and endured this one.

Still, I was uncertain of many things that night. I guess it was the night when I began to lose control or misunderstand things. Maybe it was the final waves of beer and weed sloshing at the shores of my head, but my relaxed state of mind was soon overtaken by bleary anxiety. Friday was just an aspirin for the growing headache of my future. Even as I stopped to check out the state of my own room, I felt empty, almost haunted by an ever-present need to build a future. I was sick and tired of the long prologue to a short life with a small shot at success.

I opened the closet to get dressed and was startled to find all my clothes thrown to the floor. There was a sick smell to them, as if decades of mothball dust had been stirred in the process. I stared for a moment at the clothes in their contorted, angry pile. The air was slowly seeping out of my balloon. I turned from the closet with a nervous and weary feeling. I wondered where Rosie was and what had made her this mad.

The Advocate is the name of and home to the College's literary magazine. It's a run-down two-story white clapboard house on Winthrop Street. Entering, you pass under the Advocate's seal—a Pegasus flying over the motto *Dulce est periculum*. Parties were held on the second floor in the main reading room. Despite all its riggings as a wasp nest, I enjoyed the upstairs, which is paneled with wood blocks listing each class of Advocate members. The names of Wallace Stevens, T. S. Eliot, e. e. cummings, and others are in various corners, painted in gold leaf and slowly fading into the wood. My particular favorites were the classes from the late forties and earlier fifties. Frank O'Hara, John Updike, Robert Bly, John Hawkes, Robert Creeley, Harold Brodkey, John Ashbery, Edward Gorey, Kenneth Koch—and the list just kept going. Upstairs at the Advocate was a cozy place to soak in literary value and a couple of gin and tonics.

Thoughts of Rosie pealed from my mind as I walked up the stairs to this room. She was malicious and had gone overboard. I was at the master's tea. Then again, I was starting to doubt that was the place I was supposed to meet her.

The lights in the reading room were low and the air was thick with smoke. Some ridiculous ska band was pulsing from the stereo. No one danced at these parties, but the music was always deafening. A quick check of the room revealed a few fellow Advocate members and a host of other wonderfully amiable aesthetes from the Pudding and the Signet. I breezed over to the bar and found the gin and Maeve O'Hara.

She wore a tight black velvet top exposing her midriff. A short miniskirt came down to her thighs over black tights. I noticed for the first time her dainty feet. She looked a bit like a sexed-up version of Tuesday's child. To top it off, she was more excited to see me than I could have imagined.

"You came." She stubbed out her smoke in an empty cup. "Good to see you outside of the Renaissance."

I smiled and waved my drink in a congenial manner, trying to remember how to flirt. Maeve must have had a few.

"I was telling my old roommate Lily about the class and she knew you from English Drama History."

Lily had been in my section for that class and had been a veritable minefield of cultural studies. She was very bright but the slightest comment about any male hero be it Hamlet or Faustus was quickly emasculated with a sermon on cross-dressing or how the marriage ring in comedies was a symbol of anal sex.

"How is Lily? Is she working on her thesis?"

"She took the semester off. Lyme disease or lupus, I can't remember which. She was calling from her parents' house on the Vineyard. Are you doing a thesis?"

"Yeah, Shakespeare, very original stuff."

That made her laugh a bit, which I took as a terrific sign. The both of us were soon drunk enough to talk the legs off a horse and we kept good company. Michael breezed in and out with a wink and a nod. A couple of hours passed and the Advocate was letting out for later parties. Maeve and I made sure the bar wasn't going anywhere. Her charms made me nervous in a good way. During a brief silence while the two of us stared at our glasses, I thought about Rosie. She was probably asleep or burning my possessions. Maeve's attention started to wander, and I dove into the wreck.

"I've got a bottle of tequila and a key to the Adams House roof."

She knew what all that hinted at, and Adams was not on her way home. But at this point the operative word for both of us was "tequila." She lit a cigarette, agreed, grabbed her coat, and marched me out of the Advocate.

On the way we stopped in a convenience store and got some limes. As I waited at the register, I looked over to Maeve, who was pawing through the magazine rack. She had a wick of black hair hanging in front of her eyes that gave her a coy but calm look. Again it amazed me how beautiful a woman could be when she didn't know you were watching.

We finally made it back to Adams House, and I took

the stairs to B-entry with fearful caution. As we passed the second-floor landing I heard a door unlock. I immediately tensed up. But it was just someone from the room next to Rosie's, who darted down the stairs. Maeve and I reached the fourth floor and slipped into my room. I grabbed a hammer from the bottom drawer of my desk.

"Let's head up." And I handed the tequila and salt to Maeve.

As was the case for most of our time together, Maeve was close to calling it a night with me. She surveyed my room and bookshelf and then slowly came out into the hallway. I walked over to the ladder behind the stairwell and climbed up to the roof door. There was a padlock on the door's metal hasp.

"I thought you had a key."

I brought the back of the hammer against the hasp and leveraged my weight against the door. The hasp stretched out of its bolts after a few quick pulls. The padlock slipped off the dangling hasp and fell to the landing. The lock split open—its metal springs and bearings rolling off the stairwell and crashing down the entryway. The roof door opened wide.

I climbed onto the roof, followed by Maeve, who gave me an impressed look when she reached the top. Since sophomore year I had broken onto that roof a dozen times. The security guards were too fat to climb all those stairs and the maintenance men just kept replacing one dinky hasp with another.

Maeve twirled around, pleased with our minor mischief. You could see the whole of Boston and Cambridge with the tail of the Charles winding between them. The skyline glittered to the southeast, hazing the darkness of the night into a chocolate color. The Citgo sign by Fenway Park blinked intermittently like a giant neon eye over the Back Bay. It was a fairly clear night out, but the weather needle on the old Hancock tower flashed red. The bars and cafés on Bow Street had closed hours before. Across the way, St. Paul's Catholic Church sulked in a dim corner. St. Paul's didn't fit into any architectural category except maybe creepy, guilt-laden Romanesque. The bell tower had no uplighting and rose into view as a dismal monolith. The noise of street traffic was surprisingly distant. All I could hear was the air brakes of city buses softly hissing into the night.

I poured two shots of tequila. Then I licked the hop of my thumb and poured a pinch of salt there. Maeve did the same and we toasted. I was so drunk already I barely felt the tequila's spine-warming glow. Maeve waltzed over to a far corner of the roof to look down the backs of the Mass Ave apartment buildings. I took a seat near the ledge and concentrated hard on whether to make a move or not. Suddenly the tequila kicked in. My head swung down between my knees and I could hardly think. A swath of Rosie and guilt sent me spinning. I stood up and took a deep breath, minding the edges of the roof. In the midst of my attempts to gain some composure Maeve had come back for another shot.

"You drink like a fish, O'Hara."

"It passes the time," she said, slightly leaning.

She took up the salt shaker and I despairingly raised my hand for another shot. She held back the salt for a second longer and then brought my hand to her mouth. She kissed it softly with her tongue, stood back again, and sprinkled the salt. I was in trouble. She smiled and we downed the shots. A relatively long silence ensued that was broken by a simultaneous laugh. Her eyes flickered like candles. I stepped forward and touched her chin.

"So, could I borrow your notes sometime?" I said with a false swagger.

Maeve fell back in drunken laughter. I doubled over laughing too, being sure to fall close to her. As her laugh subsided there was another silence, and I kissed her.

That first kiss was slightly open and off the mark, almost a nuzzle of chins to tell the truth. She kissed back a second later and there we were. My hand slowly went down her back and around the top of her thigh, stenciling her perfect body in my mind. She was a terrific kisser that first time, in spite of my drunken sloppiness. She was precise and coming on strong, maybe even moaning a bit. Her hand ran up my leg and pressed into my thigh with confidence.

Had I finally found a sexually aggressive—hell, responsive—woman? I was completely aroused. She pushed and pulled in subtle yet clear ways and I felt her control. I opened my eyes for a brief second and was lost in the night sky and tangles of Maeve's hair. She smelled like a broken still garnished with honeysuckle. I couldn't believe how well we hit it off and was upset with myself for not having pursued her sooner.

But we were way too drunk to do much more. After a few more minutes of kissing and handling each other, she pulled back and threw up to the side.

"Sorry," she said, pulling herself together, "but I'm about to lose it here."

This was a small death for me. Not that I was in much better shape, but this definitely put an end to the night's romance.

"Are you all right?"

"Yeah, yeah, I think I'll head home."

"Let me walk you."

"No, I'll be fine. Besides, what would Rosie think if she saw us?"

I had thought she knew about Rosie but until this point had slowly convinced myself she didn't or had forgotten or didn't care. I grinned sheepishly.

"Don't worry. I like keeping you on the edge," she said, peering over the roofside. "It's more fun that way."

I laughed nervously and watched her climb down off the roof and onto the landing.

The whole night felt so seductive and enticing that I couldn't quite get my head straight. I looked over the city smoking my last few cigarettes. It must have been coming up on four in the morning and the sky was promising the first dark blues of dawn. I was unsure what I wanted, and the night was certain proof of that. Maeve seemed fast, but maybe it was just that things with Rosie were slow. I felt like I was somewhat showing off around Maeve, but mostly I felt confident and carefully happy with myself. On the other hand, I foresaw a lot of lying to Rosie over the next few days. Making up with her for that night sickened my already drunkshot stomach. Not so much for the yelling and arguing, bad as it was, but because I knew we would eventually make up. I knew what to say and what she wanted to hear. I was fairly sure that she wouldn't suspect me of cheating yet. In Rosie's eyes we were bound to each other no matter how bad it got. Our relationship had become something to put up with. I felt like a fool—for God's sake, I had spent three years missing out on girls like Maeve. I was monogamous for all of college, and it was silly. My love for Rosie was silly. I felt trapped and wasted by it now.

The sweetness and warmth of Maeve's kisses was leaving me. A fog had begun to roll in off the Charles. I watched it carefully from my rooftop perch as it became thick as marble over the buildings and streetlights below. I felt something ignorant in that fog as it spread and blanketed over the last of the night—some vague desire to choke and clog that was unsafe, untrue. Soon its fingers crept toward the roof and collected in pockets behind the chimneys and vent shafts. The coolness of the night became damp on my face. I finished my last cigarette and moved down toward the hatch and ladder.

Suddenly a spark flared and died in the corner of my eye. I turned and peered at the far end of the roof. The empty casing of the building's discarded water tower lay in the corner resting on its side. I thought the streetlights had caught some glint of metal, but then I heard low thuds as if steps were being taken over the roof's tar paper. The noise grew louder for an instant and then ceased. Another flare of light—this time I saw it full on. My eyes were tired and my body ached for sleep but I stood there as silently as I could. My knees felt like buckling—I was frightened, cold, and not necessarily alone.

More sparks of light, this time like a subway car in a turn, but noiseless and iridescent. The fog grew thicker around the roof and I could only make out the dark line of the water tower. With each of these flashes I grew more and more accustomed to a regular motion of shadow in that corner. Instantly, the light went in two opposite directions, leaving a solid black shaft, the size of man, covering the roof corner for the briefest of moments.

The fog had now completely obscured my view and I could only make out smoky streetlamps in the distance. I held my breath and listened intensely. I turned around to view the whole span of the roof and noticed the first glimmer of dawn in the east. I stood in the cold sweat of the fog for over ten minutes and heard nothing more.

I assured myself that old pipes and pumps creak and wail as I steadily walked toward the far corner. Behind the water tower there was no one. I tried to find a piece of metal that hadn't rusted decades ago and could have created such tricks of light. Beneath the cracked joints of the tower lay a disused lightning rod. Although there was only a trace of a storm nearby I was afraid to pick it up as if that would tempt some fate. With a swift jerk, I kicked it to see if would catch light. Moving the rod, I uncovered an old book of matches. The book was red with black stripes. I opened it and found three damp matches left. I tried to read the writing on the flap, but the morning light was not strong enough. I pulled out my own lighter, struck it, and read the flap, which was an advertisement for a bar.

THE MOUSETRAP
26 Prospect Street
Cambridge
No better way to catch a cocktail.

The bar was unfamiliar to me, and I pocketed the matches. The fog had set in thick as cotton. Convinced I had spooked myself in tired drunkenness, I left the roof.

I woke up at noon on Saturday with an enormous hangover and Rosie banging on my door. I crawled off my deathbed, staggered to the door, and let Rosie in. She glared and marched right past me to the phone.

"Have you heard these messages? Because if you had you would have realized that I waited for you outside of the Brattle Theatre for an hour last night. Then I came back to Adams and waited around my room. I knew you had forgotten about the movie, but I still worried that maybe something god-awful had happened to you."

My head felt thick, like a clump of wet wool. I had totally forgotten about meeting her at the movies. "Look, I'm sorry."

"No, fuck your apology. I talked to Michael, who said you were at the master's tea until seven."

"I thought that's where we were meeting." I felt like

throwing up and turned to the bathroom. "I forgot about the movie. I'm very sorry."

"What did you do all night? Why can't you call? Why can't you check your messages? Where the hell have you been?"

Just then I remembered Maeve. The roof. The kiss. A bolt of white fear passed through me and I ran to the toilet. The vomit came like a mix of tar and acid. But I had nothing on my stomach and the throwing up soon passed into dry heaves. After three years together, I couldn't believe that I had messed around on Rosie. I finally pulled myself out of the bathroom and found Rosie sitting at my computer checking her e-mail.

"How'd that interview go?" I asked.

"I don't know. The guy from Goldman Sachs didn't drink tequila, so we had nothing in common." Her hair was pulled back in a ponytail so tight it could pop out of her scalp at any time. I was feeling much better, however, and downed half a dozen Advil. My blood ran thin from the liquor but I managed.

"Do you want to go to breakfast?" I said, trying to get on with it.

"Don't even think I'm forgetting about this. You do so well in your classes, with your teachers, your papers. Why do you have to blow things with us?"

I tensed up as it occurred to me that she had seen me with Maeve and was just leading me on. I felt guilt-ridden and ashamed. Why had I been so cavalier? I was no confidence man and Rosie was no fool. I was certain I'd get caught in a lie.

We went down to the dining hall. The fight resolved nothing, like most of our recent skirmishes. But I sipped coffee and nodded remorsefully while she ran a fork through eggs and extrapolated every facet to her being pissed off at me. I tried to eat some pancakes but the syrup was cold and had clotted into a skin. I downed several sugary cups of coffee instead.

It was still early in the afternoon and Rosie agreed to come back to my room and finish yelling at me. I also wanted her to read over my Marshall application. I had pretty much worn her out over breakfast, and hadn't betrayed anything incriminating. I told her I'd gone to the tea and the Advocate but steered clear of saying who else had been there. Rosie bristled from time to time during my explanations, but the worst had passed and I was not far from her good graces.

Back in my room, Rosie stomped around and finally settled down on my bed to look over my fellowship application. She was no farther than my date of birth before I had climbed on top of her. She was very cute when she was pissed off. It was a reaction. It felt real and I wanted to feel something with her and for her. She tensed up and thought about slapping me, but I was tender and she relented. Typical of my rather diluted fantasy life I pictured Maeve as I hid my face in the crook of Rosie's neck. I listened carefully for any signs of excitement from Rosie but after a few minutes she was starting to wince and I stopped.

I reached across the bed for a cigarette and some water. I looked around for my Zippo, but didn't see it. Rosie lay there oblivious to my presence. She was already planning out her day, dicing up her time. She was so different from when I first met her. Billy had always told me she was a pain in the ass—that it would end someday, and things should never be left to drag along. Rosie had a lot on her mind, I gave her that leeway, but she had no use for me and this distancing was proof of it. I rolled away from her on the bed and noticed the closet again, clothes still strewn across the floor.

"By the way, was this little tantrum necessary?"

"I'm not doing your laundry," Rosie replied. She got up and started putting on her bra.

"I didn't ask that. I'm asking why you had to throw all my shit on the floor last night."

"I didn't."

"Were you in here last night looking for me?"

"No."

"Then who fucked up the closet?"

"I don't know." She was ready to start yelling at me again, and I laid off it. If Rosie had done it, she would probably have felt high and mighty enough to brag about it. I got up from the bed, walked over to the closet, and pulled the door wide. Again I noticed a funny smell lingering there. The hanging bar was still in place even though everything in the closet appeared to have collapsed at once.

I started to get dressed. Rosie ran down to her room and packed up for an afternoon of studying. I filled my bookbag with a dull and steady diet of thesis readings along with my *Riverside Shakespeare*, which after my lugging it around for three years was giving me serious back pain. I packed away a pen, a highlighter, and my thesis notebook.

That's when I first noticed the pages ripped out of the notebook.

"What the hell is this?"

I desperately searched through the drawers of my desk and the piles of books. I tried to think where I could have possibly put it, but I knew I hadn't torn anything out of the notebook. There must have been five or six important pages missing. And it wasn't the crap my adviser had jawed on about; it was main citations from the reading and a fairly detailed outline of the entire thesis.

"Shit."

Rosie did it. Happy's notes went missing too. She could have gotten us both. But that made no sense. Why? I kept looking around the room, getting angrier and angrier. This couldn't be happening.

"No. No. No."

Maeve? I would have seen her. I'd never left her alone. Goddam school, enrolled with a bunch of thieves and con artists. Did they come to college to major in vandalism and backstabbing? I should have typed up those notes on the computer. At that point I was in a complete fury, throwing clothes and books across the room. Rosie walked in and yelled at me to calm down.

"Someone took pages out of my thesis notebook." I felt sick again. I couldn't decide whether to throw more things or cry. "You didn't do it, did you?"

"No, and fuck you again for accusing me." Rosie walked over to my desk to inspect the notebook. "I can't believe this. What did they take?"

"The outline, the notes from the readings." I pounded my fist into the wall. The pain jolted through my arm and throbbed there uselessly. Unbelievable.

"We should tell someone about this. First Happy and now you." Rosie wasn't quite as upset as I'd have liked her to be.

"What the hell is anyone going to do about it? It's everyone at this school. They're all a bunch of backstabbers." I sat down on the bed and held my miserable head in my hands. I was starting to calm down. Rosie was too obvious a suspect. She wasn't stupid.

"Look, it wasn't me. Why would I do such a thing?"

"Because I forgot about the movie."

"I didn't go into your room last night. I knocked, but did not go in. So just relax. It doesn't look like they took that much." She said it in a tone that almost implied that my thesis was a joke. She placed the notebook in my bookbag. "It's okay. We'll fix this. Just relax and we'll go to the library. You can write out the outline again. I'm sure you remember most of it."

I winced at the thought of having to do the work over again. It felt so damn Sisyphean and it was admitting the bastards had gotten me down. But she was right. I had to cool off. I could remember most of the outline.

"It must be some lunatic on dorm crew. We'll report it to security."

I wasn't convinced of Rosie's innocence. Maybe I should have reported her to security. But that was wrong—she was the only one who cared. She was trying to help me pick up the pieces. And come on, it wasn't the end of the world. But it was suspicious, and even if Rosie hadn't done it, she must have known that it didn't look good for her.

So we walked over to Lamont, the undergraduate library, and found a couple of easy chairs in a fifth-floor reading room. But I was in no mood or frame of mind to start reconstructing my thesis. I tried to reread an essay on Hamlet and the divided mind but found myself staring out the window. The Yard was slanted in all the obtuse, pensive light of an autumn afternoon. The clouds had cleared slightly in the west and the sunlight streaked in, a scant rainbow of oranges and light reds. The wind was blowing and the trees were full of dry rustlings. The entire Yard seemed crisp yet crestfallen in its last turn before winter.

I looked over at Rosie, who was deep into her studies. I tried to work but kept rehashing the stolen notes and the previous night with Maeve. I looked down at my thesis readings. The font size on the essays, not to mention the heavy footnoting, was minuscule and sent me into fits of despair. I finally decided to head back to Adams to shower and nap before dinner. My hangover was catching up with me and I wanted to head it off with some rest. Rosie gave me an awful look while I packed up. As I left the room she shook her head, and then went into an obvious act to ignore me.

To hell with her. I had gotten enough grief for one day. Her chastisements had turned into some sort of ceremony or dance we had to go through to justify things. It was getting to be like church.

I bolted through the exit of Lamont, crossed Mass Ave, and strolled down Bow Street. As I reached the walkway for Adams I stopped for a moment. I didn't want to sit on that bed and stare at those walls in my room. The front of Westmorely faces east and had lost its light hours ago. The house just loomed in the shadows, ready for night.

So I turned down DeWolfe Street instead of going inside. Don't ask for cues or motives. But I can tell you that I was more restless than tired that afternoon. I had some thoughts and problems to walk off.

I wasn't angry at Rosie, but I was upset about the course our relationship had taken. Granted, mistakes had been made—most of them by me—but more important, we both felt that we were missing out on something because of the other. I certainly knew her well enough. The notes were a fluke. Even if she had been the one who ran off and burned them, I had been a jerk and she was still capable of love. But, as dim-witted as it sounds, we were growing apart. At that point, it was difficult to imagine a future for myself that included her.

I reached the end of DeWolfe Street. I felt like turning right towards Winthrop House and Maeve's room but thought better of it. I headed left onto Memorial Drive.

And then there was the suspicious, cynical side to this. Rosie didn't know what she wanted either—why else would she put up with me at this stage? She too was waiting for the outcome of senior year—and stringing me along just in case. The second she landed that comfortably challenging, well-paying consulting job she'd be rid of me.

I crossed Memorial Drive and walked along the path by the Charles. I loved Rosie. The ordeals of college had given us a closeness we had both trusted until now. But it used to have mystery. She used to be beguiling. There was a pragmatism in her that kept growing and growing during the time I had known her. It's hard to explain the change in her, and it was quite gradual. She stopped laughing with me and her own sense of humor got meaner. We used to go out, but now she would lock herself away and just study. She was so set on being normal, on quelling all the rumors, that she had run herself into narrow-mindedness. But every time I thought I had lost the girl I fell in love with, she'd show that spark, that lovingness we both needed.

But now it was slipping. I didn't have the time (or even

the desire) to grab it and hold on to it. Maybe the prospect of breaking up with her had stirred up my memories of Billy. His suicide was our silent bond. Perhaps we should have talked about it and cleared the air. But we didn't. Neither of us could bring ourselves to admit our part. The guilt just hung there like stagnant air in a tomb. Time seemed to make it go away, but his memory never did. And now Rosie and I had both changed. Probably for the worse. And as the change was slow, the breakup would be a long disaster. None of this seemed for the better.

Before I knew it, I had walked a half mile beyond the campus. I looked back at the red dome of the Dunster House tower as it refracted the last of the afternoon light into a multitude of golden fibers. Across the river, the tops and corners of business school buildings peeked out from a thicket of trees. Farther back on my side of the Charles, I could make out the dark gables of the boathouse. For more than three years that school had had my unrequited devotion. Whatever I had built in my years there was bound to fall apart. For the first time in my life, I felt that I had squandered my chances.

I turned away from the College and continued to stroll along the river. The walk was getting longer and wasn't sorting out anything. I had an ulcerous tendency to panic over the same problems, solving nothing. Maeve and our revels of the previous night became a smaller and smaller part of my worries. The greatest hurdles were still to come—my thesis, the fellowship, whatever was next after college. A soft, steady breeze came in off the Charles. To my left was the old power plant—a knot of bricks and wires that churned from deep within itself. I walked alongside and came to a street cutting in behind the plant. It was Prospect.

I turned up Prospect while looking for the matchbook in my pockets. I had no particular place to go, so I thought I'd look for the Mousetrap. The bizarreness on the roof from the previous night was still mulling around inside my head like a dream that leaves its trace but not a memory of what happened. It also provided me with some relief from thinking about Rosie, Maeve, or my thesis. I was hoping that the Mousetrap might be my kind of place—a blue-collar, one-beer, one-whiskey joint.

Prospect cut through mid-Cambridge public housing and was a fairly tough, desolate street until you got to Central Square. I kept my head down searching for a pattern in the gum smacks while cars sped precariously close to my side of the curb. The cold whipped down from the river and I felt intensely lonely. After a few blocks of digging around, I found the matchbook stuck in the flaps of my wallet. The address—26 Prospect.

I continued up Prospect, Central Square now in view. The street numbers were decreasing. Between two blocks of projects, I came upon a small blacktop and playground. I had just about passed by when a basketball bounced across the sidewalk in front of me. I watched it for a moment, then, minding my own business, started crossing the street. I was dreaming answers to my many self-induced problems when I suddenly realized that an entire playground of kids was screaming at me to stop their ball. I looked back at the playground—some of the kids were just yelling, others gesturing that they were fed up. I fetched the ball from the curb and rolled it back to them. Three years of college makes one useless to children, and this pack in their inflated winter coats seemed fearless and bitter. I crossed the street and out of earshot of their wiseass remarks.

• • •

When I arrived at 26 Prospect I discovered it was no longer the Mousetrap but a bar called the Steam Pour. I was getting cold and decided to investigate. Besides, hair of the dog might be the thing I needed.

I walked inside. It was a shabby, brown place. The bar, a dark bevel of mahogany, ran along the left wall. On the right, the floor went back to a pool table and television where several old men were huddled around the BC game. The pressed-tin ceiling was a series of interlocking rectangles painted dark red. The staleness and look of the place seemed familiar. There was no one at the bar, and I moved to the front corner, away from the men in the back.

The bartender was Irish. I could tell by his blotchy skin and permanent five-o'clock shadow. He had his sleeves rolled up, and his thick, hairy arms rested softly on a notebook. He was doing a tally of the liquor bottles. I placed the matchbook on the bar and took off my coat. He came over when I scooted in on my stool. I ordered a black-and-tan and pulled the ashtray closer to me.

Then I checked my wallet, making sure I could cover. I found a couple of fives and wondered slightly where the rest of my money had gone. To the noxious ether of alcohol and smoke, no doubt. I sat with my back to the wall, giving me side views of Prospect Street and the length of the bar. A beer mirror along the right wall allowed me to watch the bartender as he waited for the Guinness to settle. An amber drop of evening light spilled over the corner of the windowsill. The street was quiet and cold. I focused in on the window and could make out the pale contour of my reflection—a clear white line that came down over my forehead and nose. The right side of my reflection was silhouetted by the television and lamps of the bar. I found my cigarettes and brought one to my mouth. My hand moved across the window reflection like a small, dark bird. I relaxed my eyes and gazed into the thin, transparent specter of myself.

The bartender returned with the pint, and my mind broke back into what was going on in the bar. The old men sat silently as the television hissed with the crowd noise of the game. I lit my cigarette and watched them for a few minutes. With the shrill of a whistle one or two of them would turn for a sip of beer. They seemed sleepy or sated, I couldn't tell which.

The bartender went back to his tally and I looked up at the wall above the bar. There were various old ads for beer. Above the cash register was a team photo of the '86 Red Sox. There was a giant brown stain over half the team and I imagined the brawl that had sent a beer flying up there.

I sat for a few minutes just warming up with the pint. I thought some about school but the bar seemed so far from it. This dingy place was another world—maybe the real world. College was such a bubble. And too full of promises. Too full of false hope.

I looked back up at the wall of kitsch. Closer towards me and above the icemaker, I noticed a yellowed poster in an old wooden frame. At the top of the poster, the words STEAM POUR came billowing out of blue-and-gray clouds. The clouds were hovering over a machine with a cast-iron mouth in the shape of a teardrop. The teardrop was supported by a multitude of cranks and cogs. I stretched across the bar to make out the lettering at the bottom of the poster. It read: "Boston, 1847. Ira Cedarbath opens the first brewery to operate solely on steam power."

In the right lower corner, inset over the machine, was a portrait of Ira examining a glass of his steam-powered Pilgrim Ale.

The poster seemed very familiar and sent a wave of unexplained sadness through me. I looked down and concentrated on the bubbles streaming down the sides of the Guinness. And then I remembered. The Steam Pour. What I'd mistaken for déjà vu was, in fact, memory. Or was it? In that instant, I was there again. I looked back up at the poster. Familiar, but muddled, confusing. The Mousetrap. Billy had wanted to go there. I dragged on my smoke, my heart beginning to pound. He thought we could drink underage here. When was that? From the TV came that larger-than-life cutaway music that goes with football and promises a set of commercials. It had been very cold. Right before spring break. We could barely walk straight down Mass Ave on the way back from Central Square. The Steam Pour. The Mousetrap.

I took a gulp of my pint. No, it wasn't that weekend. We got drunk a lot of those weekends. I closed my eyes and could feel the blood pulse behind them. The dim lights from the bar stung through the darkness of my eyelids. No, it was April, around Easter. I was confusing this place with somewhere else.

I wouldn't, I couldn't, believe it was the same bar. It wasn't our last night together. Pilgrim Ale. That mirror across from the bar. Prospect Street, low and blue from the shadows of the apartment buildings. I was shaking ever so slightly. Oh God, no. How could I have forgotten where we went that night?

I thumbed at the matchbook from the Mousetrap trying to stay calm. I could have helped him. I swallowed down the rest of my black-and-tan and called over for the bartender. He came quickly and annoyed.

"Sorry to bother you. But was this place ever called the Mousetrap?"

"I don't know, not since I've been here. That's two years." He emptied my ashtray and turned to keep an eye on the old men. His hands were pruned from washing glasses.

"How long has this bar been here?" I asked.

"It's over fifty years old. I think it was opened just after Prohibition."

"Was it always called the Steam Pour?"

He looked into the ice machine and wiped its stainless-steel front. "I don't think so. But I've only been here a couple of years."

"Do you own the place?"

"Who are you looking for, kid?"

I looked up at Ira Cedarbath, still intent on the color and clarity of his ale. "I'm sorry, I just thought I'd been here before, when this place was called something else."

"Do you want another?" He was bothered by the fact I was half his age and playing some memory game with him. I let my breath out slowly. Two of the old men were no longer looking at the television.

They were looking at me, their eyes blank and rheumy.

"No thanks," I said and forced a grin as the bartender walked away.

I stubbed out my smoke. Three seats down. That's where Billy had sat that night. I tried to block it out. No, it was closer to the bathroom door. He was laughing about something. I told him a joke. I put on my coat.

That was almost three years ago. We were drunk. I should have left him alone. Were we talking about Rosie? It couldn't be the same bar. I was asking about her. Did I tip off the two of us? No. The bars were all alike in this neighborhood. Where did we go that night afterwards? I'll stay away. She's all yours. And you are all hers.

I got up from the stool and the black-and-tan slowly bubbled up to my head. My throat felt swollen. I had been smoking too much. The cold air would clear me up. I had to sort myself out. We were fighting over Rosie. I was jealous of him. He didn't understand what I was getting at. It was between us. I don't know. All I could remember was that I was very jealous still. I shouldn't think about it anymore. I had to get out of that dank place—there was too much welling up and closing in.

I put down a five and left the Steam Pour.

Getting out of the bar made me feel better immediately. The place was just musty and claustrophobic, and I was too tired and nervous about things to keep it all in check. Those memories were still powerful—powerful and confused. Billy didn't know any better. I had talked him out of his suspicions. I walked from under the brown awning of the bar and took a few steps toward Central Square. The subway stairs teamed with people just off the train. I had to resolve things for myself. I had to forget about Billy. Everyone else had.

I strolled down a side street off Central Square that took me back to the Charles. I was still walking away from the College, but I didn't mind. Maybe I was fooling myself with hopes and expectations. No one was helping me, and only a handful of people cared. I was on my own and the best thing for everyone would be my own disappearance or failure.

I walked along for miles with no certain destination. The water of the river was a murky, impenetrable brown. I stared for a long while into it, mesmerized by the ripple and glide of wind against water. Did the water move, or was it the current? I continued walking. The river bent back towards East Cambridge. Across the water, I could now see the half shell of the Esplanade and the first outlying streets of Beacon Hill.

I concluded that I had no luck and was out of ways to make it. I had to be deliberate and not angry with myself. I couldn't allow myself to get caught up in all the fuss and jousting. Bend not break, stay mild yet confident. There was no current, no unseen force, pushing me along. I had to remember myself—I was still here, guilty or not. I had to protect myself against all things.

The river ran into its final turn. I wanted a cigarette but realized I had no matches. It was early in the evening and a Red Line train crawled across the Pepperpot Bridge into Boston. The train tracks gleamed in the setting sun. The bridge, like so much now, was heavy, gray, and burdened. No person crossing the river was ever the same. I crossed there and took the subway back home.

When I returned to Adams, I walked through the dining hall and got a cup of coffee. The dinner hour had begun, but Saturday evenings were for going out and fewer people ate in the dining hall. I then headed to B-entry and up the stairs to my room. I thought about the schoolwork that was awaiting me. With the pages stolen from my notebook I felt so behind. I skipped up the first two flights of stairs, but took the corner of the staircase too fast and ended up spilling some coffee on the third-floor landing. I was deliberating whether to clean it up when I heard a door close on the fourth floor. I was down and to the far side of the landing when it happened. I couldn't be sure with the echoes of the hall, but the noise seemed to be my door closing. I left the spill behind and climbed the stairs to the fourth floor.

As I came up, Michael stepped out onto the landing.

He seemed preoccupied for the second before he saw me. He hesitated and looked down at himself, as if to check for keys and wallet. Then he looked down the stairs, and saw me. He seemed genuinely surprised.

"I was just knocking on your door." He adjusted his backpack, sliding it farther back on his shoulder.

"Well, here I am," I said still studying him for his reasons. If he had any, he was not letting on. When was the last time he had been by my room? Had he been inside my room? I'd never given him the key, nor for that matter had I ever lost my key. I was tired and hearing things, I thought. The door shutting must have been someone else's on the floor.

"So, party boy, have you run into Rosie yet?" he asked, very much at ease.

"I have char marks from the third degree, thank you."

"You should have seen her last night when we bumped into each other." Michael started stabbing the air in front of him. "Unhealthy, very unhealthy. I thought she was going to beat me up for just seeing you."

"I know. I'm horribly whipped." I wondered where they would have had occasion to bump into each other.

Michael looked away and asked, "So how is Maeve O'Hara?"

"She's a very friendly girl."

"Get out of here."

"Nothing really happened." I lowered my voice. Rosie's room was only two floors down. "We sat up on the roof and shot Cuervo."

"Did you tell Rosie?"

"Yeah. She was happy for me."

Michael laughed. "You are so sly. I came by to find out

what you're doing tonight. Maybe we can head to the Bow later, say after ten?" Why hadn't he just called me?

"I don't know," I said looking down at my shoes. "I'm hungover to begin with. Maybe." I wheeled around on the landing to walk towards my door.

"And we have to start planning for Heaven and Hell—and the masquerave. What are you going as this year?"

He was talking about the house's annual Halloween bash. B-entry was hosting the pre-party. "I don't know," I said, giving him a smug look. "I have to talk to Rosie."

Michael smiled at that. "So how's the Marshall going?" he asked, like it was a throwaway question. We were both applying.

"I'm sick of looking at my application," I answered, playing that old game of academic rope-a-dope: downplaying expectations while quietly and rabidly cramming for the extra-credit question. I took another step toward my door, but was struck by a thought and turned back. "Michael, were you up on that roof last night?"

"No," he laughed. I glanced again at his backpack, which he kept at a distance from me. The backpack had a bulge that didn't look like books.

"I could've sworn someone was up there with us. A fog rolled in and from what I could see it looked like someone was smoking out up there."

Michael padded softly down the stairs. "Not me. I cashed out fairly early." He stopped and waved goodbye. "One piece of advice. Don't play Rosie for the fool. It'll get you paranoid and her hurt. And I bet you she'll find out."

"See ya." His words seemed almost menacing. How was Rosie going to find out? It was good advice and I should have probably taken it that way, but I couldn't help thinking that Michael was more concerned about Rosie than me. For some reason Michael was always at liberty to tell me what I was doing wrong, and where I was going to slip up. Maybe it was a quirk in our friendship, maybe he was just concerned for me, but I resented it. I couldn't help feeling talked down to.

I entered my room and listened to the door close behind me. It had a familiar creak and slam to it but that was without the open space of the hall playing with the noise. It was now completely dark outside. I needed to think things over and relax while doing it. More important, I was down to my last pair of socks and underwear and I needed to do some laundry. I gathered various articles of clothing that were strewn across the floor and threw them into a laundry bag. I even hung up the clothes in my closet, and put the worst-smelling items in with the pile to be washed. Tired and unsettled, I felt laundry would add some order to the chaos of my room. I threw the laundry over my shoulder and shuffled down the stairs. B-entry had its certain quiet gloom and the shadows were pitched in corners as if it were midnight. I reached the bottom of the stairs and headed for the tunnel that led to the laundry room. Once there I dropped the bundle of clothes into the washer and stole some detergent from the sap who always seemed to leave it out for the taking. Having not separated colors and whites, I set the washer on a cold-water cycle.

I left the laundry room feeling slightly better about things. If I just took a washed-out day and got organized, I'd be back on track. I needed to be free of distraction—whether it be Michael or Maeve, Rosie or Billy.

Realizing I hadn't eaten anything all day, I walked

through the tunnels to the dining hall. I got some coffee and a bowl of cereal and took them to the far end of the dining hall. I sat alone in the growing buzz of the dinner rush. I caught a couple of glances from the group tables. There was nothing like eating alone in the dining hall to bring out true odium for fellow classmates. If they saw a loser eating alone, I saw mindless cliques of insecure morons gloating over themselves.

The table closest to me was a typical bunch of Connecticut prep school kids with their baseball hats and flannel shirts. At the head of the table sat their leader, who wore khakis and a pullover fleece that advertised some crappy lacrosse team. I couldn't help but overhear him.

"I told the senior tutor too. But I don't think he even believes me."

"That guy's such a loser." They were all drinking milk for some reason and each of them had three or four glasses of it on his tray.

"Yeah. I left my room for ten minutes to check my laundry and it was gone."

"The laundry?"

"No, dimwit, my computer."

"What kind?"

"A laptop. All the notes for my thesis were on the thing."

I dropped my spoon in the cereal bowl. The one who was doing all the talking turned and glared at me. I didn't know him personally but he lived in B-entry. I wanted to share the story of my theft, but that would admit I was snooping. I got too nervous about it and pretended to be reading a newsletter someone had left at my table.

"I tell you this house is full of freaks." Lacrosse guy took a big gulp of milk. "I don't know where to start.

Who would do that except some klepto? And now we're talking about half the people who live in Adams."

His buddies laughed. I pushed out my chair and walked away, followed by their sniggers and stares. Bunch of stupid rich milk-drinking mama's boys. What could he possibly be writing a thesis about? The silver spoon lodged up his ass?

The coffee and food had not improved my hangover, and I couldn't decide what to do with myself. My best idea at the time was to try to lie down again. I headed out of the dining hall and back down to the laundry room. My head was pounding as the two hemispheres of my brain grated over Maeve and Rosie. I also was thinking about my latest, odd encounter with Michael and how I didn't like the sound of his answers. I felt sure he was hiding something from me. Maybe he was the B-entry burglar. But why? He wasn't the type. Then again, everyone was stressed out and acting suspicious.

Walking through the tunnel, I noticed a dark pool of water outside the door of the laundry room. At first I didn't care, because all the pipes and machines in that room seemed to leak. The washers were very old, reminiscent of the Cold War in a strange, metallic way. It wasn't until I reached the door that I realized the water was blood-red.

I stepped over the puddle and looked inside the laundry room. Red water was streaming out of a washer and spilling out onto the floor. It was the washer with my clothes in it.

I threw open the lid of the washer to stop the cycle. The water—dark as crimson but foamy with the soap—continued to cascade for a few seconds and then leveled out. I noticed that in the fifteen minutes I had been gone the other two or three people doing laundry had cleared out. I pulled out a piece of clothing to inspect—it was a sock completely soaked and dripping with red dye.

At that very moment, I heard a faint laugh echo down the hallway.

I dropped the sock back into the washer and ran into the tunnel. I turned the near corner so I was able to see both ends of the hall.

No one.

I felt like I was being watched. The red water trickled farther down the tunnel, finally finding a drain to suck it down. This had to be deliberate. Someone had thrown red dye into the washer. Someone had followed me and done this. I turned back into the laundry room, disgusted and on the verge of tears. Laughter seeped from down the hallway again, this time slightly farther away.

"Who's there?" I shouted. Strangely my voice didn't carry at all. I didn't know whether to be angry or scared. This was beyond the annoying and occasional prank.

And where was everybody else? At dinner, but it was certainly suspicious that not a soul had passed through the tunnels in the time I had been down there. Was the whole house against me? Why were they all staring me down in the dining hall? Why were they avoiding me and letting this happen?

Tears welled up and my face felt flushed. What the hell was going on?

I walked over to the washer and took out my laundry. I noticed the water felt lukewarm, not cold as I had set the washer for. I thought about rinsing my clothes out, but every piece was red through and through and had been completely ruined. As I went to throw it out, I caught a pale, scratched reflection of myself in the metal lid of the trash can. What a miserable sight. I was on the verge of tears and the red dye was running from the clothes down the length of my arms and onto my pants and shoes. It looked like I was disposing a body, for God's sake. I slammed the laundry down into the trash and turned away, sickened by it all. I started to whimper and tried to hold it back. First the notebook and now this. It was just too much. I pounded and kicked at the washer. I was full-on weeping now and the lilt of that laughter echoed in my mind—mocking me, driving me into a rage.

Something in me broke that afternoon. It was too many tough breaks to be just coincidence. I stood there in the laundry room unable to make any sense of it. I stopped crying, ashamed at my own childishness. Who could be so sick and sadistic? I was already fairly paranoid about school, my girlfriend, and others, but now greater wheels of doubt had started to spin within. At the end of my thoughts was the feeling that no one knew me, no one truly cared, and no one was trustworthy. I couldn't even trust my own memory of Billy. If it hadn't been the right bar, it wouldn't have been so unsettling—the memories of him so strong.

Something about senior year was leaving a bitter taste. Rosie, Michael, all of them were off-and-on friends set on going their own ways and without a thought for me. Not that anyone in this life owed me a damn, but I felt duped nonetheless, as if I had been tricked into caring about these people while they mined away at future success. I staggered through the tunnel to B-entry and began climbing the stairs to my room. All in all, nothing seemed to be working out, and I was sick of trying to keep the parts together.

I reached the third floor and turned up to the fourth

flight of stairs. Again, a door creaked open and then slammed. I paid it no attention until I was halfway up the stairs and saw in the corner of my eye someone leaning on the stairwell. I didn't focus on this person, but it was a man, rather tall, wearing a jacket and tie. I took another step up the stairs. He shifted his weight from one side to the other.

All of this I can recall from the briefest of moments because of what came later. My mind was elsewhere that afternoon but this was another point where I can begin my explanation. Another time when I was played into the deck. Another thing I could not prove.

When I looked up at the landing a second time there was no one there.

I was startled and stopped in the middle of the flight of stairs. Sounds in the hallway could easily be deceiving but the dim lighting was at its most in the middle of the landing. I stood motionless for several seconds, my eyes darting to and fro across the hall. I felt very tired and distracted. I walked up the rest of the stairs still looking and listening around the fourth floor for any sign of life. I reached the top of the stairs. The whole entryway was unusually quiet and empty of people. I could smell cigarette smoke but it may have been my own clothes. I turned to my door and through the stillness I listened to my footsteps echo down the hallway. I looked back once more but saw no one.

Anyone can fool himself into fear but at that moment the silence left me unsettled and expectant, like watching someone forcefully holding his breath. There was something about the landing that absorbed all the white noise and drew attention to itself. As I put my key to the door, I could hear the springs pop up in the lock. I jiggled with the key but the latch wouldn't open. I placed my foot against the door and pulled the key up and towards me, trying to find the trick to unlock it.

I felt something move across the landing and looked behind me. I saw and heard nothing. Without reason, I was convinced someone was there, and I jiggled the key more frantically. Within the noise I created, I could hear faint footsteps and laughter from down the stairwell. Finally the door flew open from the lodge of my foot. I could feel the air collapsing at my back as if somebody was closing in fast. Waves of dread shivered down from my neck. I ducked in behind the door and slammed it shut. As the door closed, I heard a whisper carry across the landing:

Except my life, except my life, except my life.

I stopped and listened at my door for several minutes. There was only silence. As my fear dissolved, my paranoia grew. That whisper echoed in my head for the days and nights following. I kept wondering, who? Who would do this? I felt uneasy, as if someone were out to get me. Who was trailing me in the halls, destroying my notes and laundry, and smoking silently on the roof? Was it Rosie? What did Rosie have on Maeve and me? And why had she thrown a total conniption in my closet and then denied it?

But I wasn't going to find answers to these questions. At that point, I didn't know what the real questions were.

At the College there seemed to be a fine line between thinking everyone was out to get you and that actually being the case. Paranoia cut everything both ways. Michael was my friend but I knew he was also applying for a Marshall. Maybe he had me going in order to distract me and keep me out of the running. Then again, Michael had always liked Rosie, and I saw how she looked at him. Maybe Rosie was colluding some sick revenge with Maeve.

So I knew I was being paranoid. But I also wanted to play it safe around the angles. What else could I do, surrounded by all those overachieving nitwits? I wished I were less skeptical, but everyone seemed self-centered enough to screw you over. At the same time, such selfishness would most likely prevent Michael, Rosie, and Maeve from acting together. The three of them conspiring together was hardly likely. If they were up to something, one of them would rat the others out at the slightest suspicion on my part.

Even though three years had passed, I couldn't help but think of Billy's hand in all of this. In a way, my college life had been spent getting out from under the shadow of his death. I shouldn't have felt guilty, but I did. The more I tried to forget, the more I felt cursed by him.

Rosie and I never talked about Billy's suicide, but we did feel haunted by his death. He was a good, honest friend and we had betrayed him. I can't remember much about him anymore, but I do recall waking up in the middle of the night early freshman year to Rosie and him having sex in the bed next to me. I was annoyed, of course, but more than that, I wanted Rosie and she seemed to be teasing me with Billy. Many times when Rosie and I were having sex, I thought of Billy in this way. I had usurped him.

So when the hallway's sounds and shadows started

playing tricks on me, other suspicions took hold. I was guilty of betrayal, and there was no way I could ever redeem myself. I was almost certain he had had no idea, but then at the bar, his presence and my memories started to come back. The pain came back, and the guilt and loneliness too. Maybe he had known. The confusion just made me more fearful and I fully expected that Billy, or someone, was watching.

The third week in October descended into hell. On Monday and Tuesday I was incessantly unprepared, late, or absent from class. Rosie was in New York for recruiting interviews until Wednesday. I didn't see Michael either. He must have been over at his girlfriend's apartment in Davis Square cramming for midterms. All the same I was avoiding people, especially professors and teaching assistants. I turned in my first round of papers an average of a week late. I couldn't study and couldn't catch up on my sleep either. I tried to rewrite the outline for my thesis, but I just couldn't concentrate. Instead I stayed up all night tapping away at Tetris or staring out my French doors at the neighboring traffic lights. My floor was covered with books left open from where the thesis reading had stopped weeks ago. My stomach started to burn into an ulcer with tension over the thesis.

This thermidor of a god-awful semester hit its worst on Tuesday night when I gulped down a bottle of NyQuil and wandered down into the tunnels of Adams House to play pinball in the laundry room. I could barely walk straight, and after blowing several games I permanently tilted the pinball machine and curled up on a washing machine to sleep. At one point, somebody unloaded a dryer, but I pretended not to notice. I just drifted off on the smell of detergent and softener. I woke up several hours later, my hangover well under way. The whine of the fluorescent lights pierced my head. I went back to my room in tears, sick of myself and my ineptness. I crawled into bed and lay there hungry, tired, half awake, and half doped up.

A phone call broke this spell of depression. The answering machine clicked on. It was Michael. He wasn't named a finalist for the Marshall. And neither was I.

"Well, friend, I guess we won't be punting together on the Cam or the Avon. Give me a call and let's drown our sorrows."

I fell out of bed. It was nine in the morning, so I went to the dining hall. Maybe I didn't need the fellowship. Maybe it was a sign—a bad break that would free up the time to put some pieces back together. I got a cup of tea and read the College paper. On the front page, below the math club's latest stunning upset, four Marshall finalists from the College were listed. I had believed Michael's message, but seeing the names of the others who had made the cut brought home the failure.

I looked up from the paper, wounded by the news. After a few minutes, though, I was stung but surviving. My application had been as good as anybody else's, the process was exacting, and there were a hundred reasons for getting the award and a hundred reasons for being rejected. A sense of calm pervaded my exhausted head. I was running through the hurdles rather than over them. But at least, I rationalized to myself, I knew what was not an option. Part of me was free by failure and default.

I returned to my dreary and confining room. I wanted

to get out and go somewhere, but was too tired to move. I decided it best to recover and pull myself together. I walked over to my desk, shuffled through the rat's nest of papers, and produced a copy of my Marshall application. I lay down on the bed and began to read.

I should have come up with a more original plan of study than Shakespeare. It had been done. Then again, it was a huge challenge to tackle a subject that large. Every detail to the application could be second-guessed—the committee was known for being snide and moody about the slightest thing.

A few sentences into my first essay, I caught a spelling mistake. I swore out loud to myself, but the curse only echoed in my own ears. It was a chilling reminder of how alone I was. I listened for a moment. B-entry was completely still. The fourth floor of B-entry suddenly felt like a far-out Atlantic lighthouse on some forgotten, fog-laden blast of rock. And the storm clouds were gathering.

I kept reading and soon found another mistake—a misplaced modifier. How could I have not caught that? I had read this essay a hundred times. I skipped ahead to the second essay—how would you describe yourself? It was the kind of bullshit question that I loved. I would make up some recently deceased relative and give the usual sob story of how their outlook changed my life. In fact, over a career of writing personal essays I had composed an entire imaginary family. An uncle who through baseball taught me that life wasn't all about winning. A grandmother whose piety and community service showed me how to be a man for others. And a "life is short" cousin who died in some tragic circumstance, most often a boating accident or cancer. Sure it was deceptive, but I was competing against people who worked in leper colonies and dug latrines in every possible third-world country. Wasn't the lesson learned authentic enough, even if I was never actually taught it?

But as I started reading the second essay I was shocked at what I found. The grammar was lousy. It made no sense. I checked the first page to make sure it was the final draft. I didn't even remember writing half of this gibberish. I scanned down to the third and final essay—describe your course of study. It was equally awful. Misspellings everywhere—"Halmet," "metapysical." Completely embarrassing.

Disgusted, I threw the application down to the floor. What was I doing turning in this shit? I must have printed out an earlier version and accidentally submitted it. The idea of that mistake began to blister inside me. How stupid. What a waste of time. I had a pounding headache and reached for more NyQuil. It was all gone. I dug around in the bathroom and eventually found some pain pills left over from the extraction of my wisdom teeth. I took four and returned to my desk.

There I found my thesis notebook and a couple of essays my adviser had photocopied for me. I took these all back to bed, kicking the Marshall application across the room and out of sight. I plopped down and began paging through my thesis notebook, trying to make sense of the ever-growing pile of work that had to be done. I couldn't believe that I hadn't written a single word of the actual thesis. And after losing the outline, I was seriously screwed.

I noticed the torn-out pages of the notebook. I was about to get angry again when it dawned on me. If someone had taken those, why not tamper with the application? Michael immediately came to mind. Maybe he had a crush on Rosie, but I knew for certain he wanted a Marshall. I was beginning to feel dizzy. But why pick on me over a Marshall? It was too ridiculous. But what if he had Rosie's help? I had forgotten how strong these pills were. Who was I kidding? It was my own stupid mistake. Nothing was going right, and each step I took was a bigger disaster than the last. The pain pills were overtaking me. Suddenly it felt as if a warm light were being waved over my body. I let the thesis notebook slip from my hands. I closed my eyes. My throat was very dry and I needed a glass of water. I was about to get up for it when I passed out completely.

I slipped into a very cold dream.

I was walking down Mass Ave headed towards the Square, but still some ways off from the College. The dream seemed very real, and I realized that was because it was something I was partly remembering—something I was almost rehearsing and trying to figure out. It was freezing—the wind funneling around street corners and stinging my face and hands. My old frayed peacoat—a holdover from high school—was providing little help. Even the glow of a few beers was fading quickly.

I looked ahead. It must have been pretty late, because I hadn't seen another soul on that walk back to the College. Cars groaned by occasionally, but their noise felt like a kind of absence. My hands were quite numb.

Then I saw someone across the street and slightly ahead of me. From that instant, the dream took on a kind of order. It was Billy trudging through an unshoveled sidewalk of ice and snow. I called out to him, but it only made him walk faster.

I crossed the street and tried to catch up to him. I could sense his anger, but couldn't remember what I had told him or what he knew. It was too cold to think. The numbness crept on me further. All I could feel was guilt. Yes, I felt very guilty and very foolish.

"Billy, come on. You don't understand." The words came from nowhere. Even as I dreamt, I knew this was a memory being played out in the hope of correction, but then falling again and again into the same futile trap.

Billy didn't turn around. "Just get away from me." He crossed Prescott Street and turned up toward the Freshman Union. I followed a few steps behind. He didn't know. That's not what this was about. He was just pissed off that I blamed him for our friendship unraveling. A couple of drinks and I let him have it.

"Stop, Billy, I was just kidding."

"Bullshit." He stopped and turned around. I think he was starting to cry. "Don't think I don't know what's going on."

"What are you talking about? Take it easy."

"Why are you always blaming me? Why are you so fucking petty? You and Rosie—it's like the two of you are against me."

A tear ran down his face.

"Look, I'm sorry for what I said." Don't ask me what it was, I felt like I was reciting lines—a performance in déjà vu.

His eyes darted back and forth suspiciously. "What you said. More like what you did." He turned and walked into the Yard muttering something about missing his midterms.

"What did I do?"

But I knew all too well. The question was did Billy know. I let him walk off for a few paces and then I yelled that I was sorry. He buried his head in his hands and started running off. The wind blew up sharply and I nuzzled my chin into my coat as I watched him. I felt at a loss to fix things. I shouldn't have let him go off alone, but I did.

I turned back toward Mass Ave and walked to a coffee shop in the Square. I thought it best to give him some time to cool off. I had never seen Billy like that, and I thought he was blowing things way out of proportion. Freshman year had lost its newness and the stress had set in on all sides—his classes, his girlfriend, and his blabbering, backstabbing roommate. But all I did was point out how close we used to be and how things were straying. He just resented the whole subject. He had this huge chip on his shoulder. I wasn't in charge of setting his alarm and making sure he got up in time for midterms. I wasn't Billy's keeper.

I sat in the coffee shop for half an hour. There was more I just couldn't admit it to myself: Billy was seriously hurt. He had to know. The wind howled against the door as I went to leave. Hard to believe it was the first night of spring break. The Yard was empty and ominous. I should have gone home for break. I was part homesick and part tired of the place. I crossed through the gate and made my way towards Matthews Hall.

I had to put a stop to the Rosie situation. I had betrayed a friend, and that—not the coldness of a dream mixed with memory—was where the numbness came from. I had to admit a small part of me wanted to tear them apart, and it wasn't like Rosie wasn't willing. Nonetheless, I had to mend things between Billy and me. At the time, there was no future with Rosie, even if I wanted her.

I climbed the stairs of Matthews. The dorm was unnervingly quiet with everyone gone on break. I was so messed up that I couldn't admit to myself the real reason I had slept with Rosie. But it didn't matter then. I had to put it all past us. Billy was my best and only friend. I had to save that.

I reached the door to our fourth-floor room and was surprised to find it locked. I took it as a mild indication that Billy was still pissed. Maybe he hadn't come home at all. My hands were so cold and raw that I could barely grasp the key. The long walk home had worn me out, and I felt a heavy tiredness coming on. I unlocked the door and turned the knob.

The door wouldn't open. I leaned against the door and checked the lock. Something from inside was holding the door closed. How goddam immature. What kind of antics were these? What could he be thinking? I pushed hard at the door, and I could hear the legs of a chair screech against the wooden floor. After a few more shoves, the door opened wide enough for me to slip through.

The room was very dark except for a yellow light flickering from the fireplace. We had started the fire in the early evening and now it was down to a few glowing embers. They had turned off the heat in the dorms over the holiday, and with the fire out, the room was very drafty. I stepped into the common room and called Billy's name.

No response.

I came into the center of the common room and watched the dim shadows of the embers dance across the far wall and drawn shades of the window. The room was cold but quiet, and I left the lights off. Billy was probably asleep and I didn't want to disturb him. I was angry, but maybe it was best to sleep on it. Even in a dream, time seemed to heal most wounds.

But the peace of the room wasn't sinking in. This was still my fault. Billy had ignored me, and yes I was jealous of him. And God knows what I was doing with Rosie. That was something I couldn't explain. It had to stop. I had to stop. The guilt pooling like an inky nothing inside me. I crept toward the bedroom to change. I was going to sleep on the couch and leave Billy alone. The door to the bedroom was slightly open. I took a step in. Pitch blackness and my eyes took a few seconds to adjust. It was so cold, my arms and legs so numb. There was a Bible on his bed but Billy was not there.

In my dream, I tried to imagine where he could be. I knew, but the dream had to take. I had to run that nauseous, fateful wheel. Each action, each thought deliberate and fated. Oh where could he be? Maybe over at Rosie's. The possibility made me nervous. Then again, Rosie had more to lose by telling him. Unless what I secretly feared was true—Rosie had been trying to get Billy away from me all along.

I went from the bedroom to the bathroom. How many times do I have to live this? The numbness was thorough, deadening. The words of an old song came to me as I walked across that dim, wintry room. *This heavy heart I carry. This heavy heart . . .*

Now I knew where Billy was. He was hanging from the shower curtain rod.

I woke up with a fever, my body shaking.

I was late for my meeting with my thesis adviser.

I left Adams in the blink of an eye and dashed across the Yard to Warren House and the offices of the English department.

The house is a sagging three-story Victorian with a wide black porch that droops into the walkway. Professor Henry Warren, the college's first professor of orientalism, was its former owner. While the ground floor had its normal run of sitting and drawing rooms, Professor Warren rarely climbed down the stairs. As a child, the professor had been thrown from a carriage, injuring his spine and permanently crippling him. The second and third floors exhibit evidence of his handicap. The study on the second floor, now inhabited by four professors, has a hidden bed under the slope of the stairs where Warren would rest in the afternoon and was able to work from his knees. He died quietly in this room at the age of forty-five.

Across the hall was the dining room, now the faculty conference room. The blackened hearth and wall panels are trimmed with Turkish tiles. The room is encircled by a third-floor balcony. In his last few years, Professor Warren would perch himself on this balcony and watch over his family's meals and social gatherings. He preferred to hover and lurk in this way—giving him the benefit of being in the room while just watching at the same time.

My thesis adviser's office was on the second floor adjacent to the main bath, which houses Warren's gigantic dark green cast-iron tub. What must have been an original attempt at a shower fixture hangs precariously above the tub, giving the small room a dank, contagious atmosphere.

I popped through the front door of Warren House and raced up the creaking stairs to the second floor. I listened at my adviser's door before I knocked and heard his voice lilting up and down in conversation. After all my panic I was only fifteen minutes late. I figured he was on the phone and knocked softly at the door. I heard his chair roll forward across the wood floor. He opened the door, welcoming me into his office. He had not been on the phone and there was no one else in his office.

My adviser was a twenty-seven-year-old doctoral candidate in the department. I had been assigned to him after my junior tutorial and had been told by my fellow English majors that I was very lucky with the pairing. My adviser was something of a hotshot in the department. There were rumors that his dissertation, which he was now in the fourth year of working on, was to rewrite the book on Lear and incest themes. I felt fortunate to have an adviser who shared the same focus as my thesis, even if he did talk to himself.

Unlike most graduate students, my adviser was well-groomed, always wearing a dark sports jacket and a collared shirt or turtleneck. He was unusually tan for the time of year and his dark hair was slicked straight back. A slightly hipper version of the black-framed glasses worn by Groucho Marx anchored his whole face. On the street, he was no looker, but among academic gerbils, he was considered an Adonis. Wide-eyed female students were the vast majority occupying his office hours.

This was to be our third meeting, and the first two had gone rather well. I had given him the thumbnail idea for my thesis and he had told me what criticism to read. By the end of the second meeting, though, I had the uneasy suspicion that I was reading for someone else also doing a thesis on Shakespeare.

"So did you find the Empson essay?" he asked, swinging his chair back behind the rickety desk. As a junior member of a department filled with tenured dinosaurs, he was understandably low on the ego and perks chain. My adviser's office was really a cleaning closet tucked under the eave of the second-floor roof. In the middle of the room was a very small oriental carpet with an intricate red pattern. In the back corner were several stored cases of sherry reserved for the aforementioned dinosaurs.

I slouched into a chair across from him, rolling my backpack from my shoulder onto my lap. As I got situated, I wondered why he had been talking to himself. His desk was piled with books that were going on three-year library loan. I imagined he talked to those books as he thumbed over their pages. They were his only company over the long afternoons. Above his desk was a quote from Keats's "Endymion" that seemed nonsensical to me out of context. As happened with most grad students, the years of esoteric study had left him near-blind and with a peculiar set of priorities and in-jokes.

"Yes," I replied, somewhat deflated. I had found the essay but had fallen asleep the previous night on page two.

"Good. I think you'll agree that ambiguity is integral to the middle style." He pronounced the word "integral" as if it were a brand of Goodyear tire.

"But"—I saw a chance to elude discussion about the essay and grabbed it—"ambiguity occurs throughout all of the plays, early, middle, and late."

My adviser frowned slightly then. "It comes down to doubleness and differences in metaphor and conceit." He seemed truly puzzled with my ignorance. "Didn't we cover this already?"

I knew what he was talking about in the narrow sense, but I couldn't see how it related. Then again, this was all becoming narrow and trivial.

"We have to concentrate on the deep myths and the Freudian plays," he continued. "When Hamlet is so-called 'mad,' he does this analysis himself. The language he uses edifies and undermines what the other characters understand about him."

I squirmed quietly in my chair. Was that what this was all about? Double meanings that contradict each other? The whole study of criticism was based on two answers, or even better, infinite interpretations, none of them complete, none of them right. I had tried so hard in my papers and discussion to avoid this kind of doubletalk.

That was the problem.

"You brought up *Hamlet* and I have a question about that," I said, again deflecting. My adviser picked up his coffee mug, a bit disappointed that I had interrupted him while he was on a roll. "When the ghost speaks to Hamlet, unlike, say, the witches in *Macbeth* or the auguries in *Caesar*, the ghost pretty much spells out an order of events."

I could see my adviser coming down off his astral plane of literary consciousness to address my rather obvious and trite point. He pulled off his glasses and wiped them smugly with a tissue. He acted like a chessmaster with mate in two who couldn't be bothered waiting for the novice to see it. I was annoyed and, at the same time, intimidated by him—he was going to be reading the thesis, after all.

"Two things. First, the ghost's story is never proven. The play to catch the king and the overheard prayers of Claudius *are* ambiguous and don't correlate with the ghost's story. Second, the ghost doesn't exist."

"Doesn't exist?" I looked up from my scribblings in the notebook.

My adviser let out another sigh. "Yes. You see, the ghost is a projection of Hamlet. It's wish fulfillment, plain and simple. The fear of the other that lies within ourselves."

Suddenly my head began throbbing in pain. All of his jargon began to accelerate and collide in my mind like a growing snow of static on the television. Doesn't exist? What was he talking about? My headache was becoming so strong that I could barely keep my head up to face him. I slumped back in my chair, my head in my hands.

"Are you getting this?" he asked, sensing a pinprick out of my endless needles of frustration. He put his glasses back on to take a good look at me. "Are you all right?" he further inquired.

The pressure in my temples was blinding. "What do you mean, he doesn't exist?" I said very angrily. My adviser rolled his chair behind his desk, taken aback by this last statement. He could see I was fighting off something, but he confused my pain as struggling with his argument.

"No, he does exist on a certain level, but the situation is overdetermined—"

"The ghost is in the goddam play!" I blurted with a raised voice. "How is anything ambiguous if he does or does not exist?" My head was now down towards my knees as if I was preparing for a crash or a tornado. *Till the foul crimes done in my days of nature are burned and purged away.* I tried to think through the headache, but all I could do was stare at the figures in the carpet tracing the beginning and end of the simple maze they made.

My adviser was silent. He turned to his desk and sorted his dissertation reading into different piles. He stared at a picture of the Bard he had pinned to the wall over his computer monitor. After a prolonged pause, he told me that my outline and chapter would be due in a few days, and he sheepishly suggested that I read the Empson article again for next time.

My headache ceased for a moment and I looked up from my lap. I apologized and tried to explain that I felt under the weather. He also apologized for not noticing, but I could see the insincerity in his face. I could tell that from here on in he saw me as his inferior and not as a willing disciple. And what did he know besides how to talk circles? Ambiguity was only so academics could be right all the time. Our tutorial was now an ordeal, a requirement for both of us. My thesis would be a trifle worthy of a gentleman's C adjusted for grade inflation.

Our hour came to an end. He reminded me that my thesis outline and sample chapter were due on Friday. I hurried from his office and nearly fell down the stairs on my way out of Warren House. I felt cursed, my thesis an albatross.

By the time I returned to Adams, though, I had broken out of my catatonic state and my headache was gone. I couldn't believe I had snapped at my adviser that way. The little things—the notebook, the laundry, the looks—were just smoldering in me. But I had to diffuse those tensions, and spend every waking moment of Wednesday and Thursday on my thesis.

Rosie's sister, Carrie, was in town. Like the rest of Rosie's family that I had met, Carrie was humorless and barely tolerant of me, and by no means went out of her way to ingratiate herself or be pleasant.

On Wednesday evening, I ate a hasty dinner with Rosie and then she and Carrie went off to see a movie in Alewife. Over the past few days Rosie had given me a brief pardon and shred of sympathy in light of my failure with the Marshall. Our feelings for each other, however mixed, still tried for love. She was still a caring person. Her amity, though, was evaporating proportionally to her own hard luck: her trip to New York bore little fruit and so far, the titans of consulting and banking had given her no second-round recruiting interviews.

The next forty-eight hours passed in a blur as I pounded out a ten-page outline and fifteen-page sample chapter for my thesis. The process was excruciating for the simple reason that I couldn't come up with a real thesis from the material. I had the right secondary sources and passages from the plays, but as the Friday-by-five deadline loomed I was missing all the connections.

Then on that bleary Friday morning I got it: the ornateness and convolution of the language in Shakespeare's middle style was the key signal of his turn from a playwright of comedy to one of tragedy. You start with *Romeo and Juliet*, which is a comedy that has a slapped-on tragic ending and you march steadily until you reach plays such as *Measure for Measure*, which is a comedy spun out of dire, or tragic, elements. *Hamlet*, the quintessence of this middle period, balances the two impulses of the playwright in a feverish, cosmic-joke sort of way.

It wasn't genius, but it was fairly well-founded and enough to dash off the chapter with. By four on Friday afternoon I was done typing and with five minutes to five I was proofing one last time on my way to Warren House. I red-lined a couple of errors not caught by the spellcheck and crammed the papers into my adviser's mailbox.

I walked out of Warren House like a prisoner of war being set free. I had been working on a total of six hous of napping over the past two days, and was exhausted in a mild, endorphined way. I waltzed over to the Adams House dining room and ate a bowl of stale cereal. The good news was that Rosie was going into Boston with her sister and I had Friday night to myself. I went back to my room and pissed around for a couple hours, reading and cringing at parts of what I had just turned into my adviser. It didn't matter, though; it was done. A finished thesis was forty-odd pages away.

Around eight, I pocketed my pipe and headed over to Michael's room.

"Where have you been, friend?" he greeted me.

"It smells like the flora in here."

His room was Long Island meets world music with Marley and Islanders posters hung side by side. Michael was from Massapequa, where he had been a state wrestling champ and valedictorian. He was one of the brightest people I ever knew, and I wished the competitive crap hadn't strained our friendship. We were so alike—except that Michael was a little more put-together, a little sharper than I wanted to give him credit for. But that was nothing to get upset about. When all was said and done, I didn't trust Michael completely, but he was fun to hang out with. We had been friends for a long time because of what we shared in common. In fact, Billy had introduced us freshman year, probably thinking the same thing.

"Grab a beer," he hollered as he sifted through his desk drawer for the bag.

"I brought my pipe if you want."

Michael brought the bag over to the coffee table, stopped for a moment, excused himself, and then retreated to the bathroom. You'd think that after three years of rewarmed dining-hall slop, we'd have stomachs of iron. The opposite was true.

I took the time to look around Michael's room. I glanced over the bookshelves and saw all the same books I had. We had taken so many classes together. I walked around by the couch. I was about to sit down when I noticed his backpack lying against the far side of the coffee table. Curious for no real reason, I walked over and found the zipper was undone but the bag lay closed.

I took a quick peek. Michael's backpack had a gallon container of bleach in it.

"You want to do my laundry?" Michael was standing outside the door to the bathroom.

"Sorry, I'm hypersensitive to the smell of bleach." I turned away and sat on the couch, ashamed at getting caught.

Michael shook his head as if buying my line. He stooped over and opened his mini-fridge. "Yeah, some asshole dyed all my laundry. I am so sick of this place."

I believed him. Someone was setting us all against each other. I told him the same thing had happened to me. He hesitated for a second, and the comment seemed to raise his suspicions of me more than anything else.

"That's crazy, huh?" Then he tossed me a can of beer. "I could only get that fancy stuff you hate." We both laughed. The great thing that endeared Michael to me was our common love of this horsepiss beer called Drummond Brothers, which, if we couldn't find it in the Dumpster behind the liquor store, ran for $5.99 a case. Michael also seemed to be suffering a downspell, and the two of us were fairly miserable company. I almost told him about what had happened outside my front door, but thought better of it. My eyes kept darting over to look at his backpack. Michael didn't have much to say for himself. We were a bit bored—it was the dog days of the semester—but after a few bowls and beers, our spirits had picked up tremendously.

Then Michael's girlfriend came over. Neither of them had eaten that night, so we walked over to the Tasty for a quick hamburger. The three of us were high as kites and joking about every little thing. For the moment, I couldn't be suspicious of Michael. He acted that night like a true friend and our mutual Marshall rejection had cooled the competitiveness between us.

The Tasty was the last remaining hole-in-the-wall freak show in the increasingly gentrified and Disneyfied Square.

No one looked at you or talked to you there, especially the cook, who chain-smoked over a griddle that had had its last degreasing during the Nixon administration. The old Formica counter was flecked with grease spots and cigarette burns. Most of the time what you got was in the ballpark of what you ordered.

For no apparent reason the jukebox at the Tasty was always playing *London Calling*. Michael and his girlfriend had happy Buddha smiles when their burgers came up. At the opposite end of the counter, two kids with thick Dorchester accents and many piercings were starting to throw punches at each other. The cook went after both of them with a charred spatula. I put out my smoke and headed toward the door.

"I'll be right back. I'm just going over to the newsstand while you eat."

The air outside was cool compared to the thick, greasy wafts of the Tasty. The Square was bustling with street performers and holding its normal quota of runaways, skaters, hippies, and derelicts. I strolled across to the newsstand and, God bless all us sinners, there was Maeve skimming the magazine racks. I snuck up on her.

"Excuse me, do you carry adult magazines?"

Her wide, startled eyes quickly sharpened into upside-down smiles, "Hey you, what's up?"

"It's real good to see you." I opened a fresh pack of cigarettes and tried to play it cool. I was very happy to have run into her like this.

"Are you low already? Christ you're a lush."

"Jealous?"

She laughed, and it gave off this fantastic vibe. In the blazing lights of the Square her skin looked soft and golden.

"What are you up to?" I asked.

"Taking a break from a paper." She raised the cup of coffee she was holding.

"A paper? It's Friday night."

"I know, but I'm going away on Sunday and I have my thesis and an application for . . ." She trailed off and looked away. She must have realized I hadn't made the cut for the Marshall.

"What's your paper on?" I asked.

"Turn of the Screw."

"I'll give you the one I wrote last semester. Let's get a beer." I figured Michael and his girlfriend would do fine without me.

And so I took her to the Bow and Arrow and again we had the best time getting stinko together. The night passed quickly into morning and I suggested we head back up to the roof for another round of tequila. The idea sent a warning blip across her radar.

"I don't like B-entry too much, especially after throwing up there."

"Please, you're making too much sense. Have another drink."

"No, I'd better go." Her lips were buttoned and her eyebrows raised haughtily over her pint. She was full of fake seriousness.

"Come on, you can do that paper in the morning."

"Maybe you could help me then."

"What?"

"I'm going home." But she had a big silly smile on her face, and after some more coaxing, she agreed. We climbed to the fourth floor of B-entry. The lock on the roof door was still busted and just as I was about to climb to the top, Maeve grabbed my leg from below on the ladder.

"Let's go to your room."

Naked, she was completely as I had pictured her. Her skin was pallid and smooth and her hips and breasts came back in a gorgeous set of curves. I took her into my arms. I couldn't believe what was happening, and even more incredibly, that she was so into it. I was once again too drunk to make many moves, but I was also relaxed enough to let her lead. She kissed me softly and then moved down. With each touch, she grew quicker and harder. She squeezed the back of my thigh, surging the blood forward. I was out of my league. Maeve was a complete shark and I was the remora along for the ride.

The sex was rough but that's as rough as I ever got with her. She started with small bites against my chest and neck. She straddled me and worked us into a frenzy. I sat up to face her on the edge of the bed. We moved faster and she started pounding with her fists and digging her nails into my shoulders. I grabbed her arms and held them back against the small of her back. She pretended to struggle, but wanted to be held that way. Then I lay back down, bringing her upper body down toward mine. We were now face to face, low to each other, where I could control the rhythm. She was getting very excited and grabbed a fistful of my hair. I, in turn, ran her hips down over mine, spreading her, going deeper. I was ready to explode, but I kept it going. I went forward to kiss her but she bit me hard on the lip. I rolled her off me and quickly turned on top of her. She didn't let go of my shoulders but pressed my head into her chest. In the whole maneuver to get on top, I didn't leave her, but came further towards her. Each touch punctuated with her cries. Even with a tinge of Rosie on my mind, the sex was devastating and miraculous.

Minutes later we were holding each other near and I was mindlessly tracing the stripes and boxes of the streetlights coming in against the ceiling. Maeve had a modest look in her eye and it was probably the only time I ever saw her hesitant or uncomfortable. I smiled, hoping that the look was a sign that she was melting into me. I was half worried and half happy that she wasn't my girlfriend. She was beautiful and carefree and I wanted her to love me. I sat back in the bed unsure what to say to her. Just when I had caught my breath and started to relax, there was a sharp pounding at the door.

Fear like a thunderclap rolled through me, and both Maeve and I froze for several seconds. More knocks at the door. Still naked, I hopped over Maeve and ran towards the door, afraid that if it was Rosie she might try her key. I held the doorknob for several seconds and listened. The hallway seemed still. Maeve meanwhile raced to grab her clothes. I ran down the hallway to the bathroom and pulled a towel around myself. I was scared beyond my next thought, but for a second I had to stop and laugh at how completely sitcomish this all was. Finally, I pushed Maeve towards the bathroom and went back to the door, pretending to be on the way to the shower. I was a step away from the door and could barely breathe. Three more quick knocks and the doorknob started to turn.

I had little hope of not getting caught, but at the time I

thought I could piss Rosie off with some rude comment and turn her away at the door. I could hear Maeve pull the shower curtain around her. There was a shuffling in the hallway outside the room and then the rattle and chime of keys falling to the floor. If Rosie came into my room I was done for—I didn't know where the condom was on the bed and I was certain the place smelled of weed and other things. My mouth was dry, my hands clenched. I caught the doorknob just as it came to a full turn. I swung open the door towards me.

There was no one there. I poked my head out into the hallway and still saw nothing. At the far right corner of the landing I could see the door to the roof was open and swaying against the wind. The hinges of the roof hatch creaked softly but otherwise I heard nothing.

Momentarily relieved, I stepped back into my room. I stared out into the hallway one last time. I was about to close the door when in the corner of my eye I saw a small piece of paper under the outer doorjamb. I looked more closely and the paper turned out to be a playing card—the jack of hearts. I picked up the card and threw the door closed, locking it shut.

Back in the room, I couldn't contain myself. Trucks of paranoia ran me down. I tried to sit and had to get up. Standing, I was able to put on a button-down shirt and some jeans until I felt my head swim and drain. I looked down at the playing card clutched in the palm of my hand. The jack of hearts grinned back at me. Maeve, I believe, came out of the bathroom fully dressed and quietly moved to the door. I could barely speak and what I saw of her was a blur. Sensing my breakdown, she blurted some final words, something about the night being so crazy, and left quickly.

The moment she was gone, I fell to the foot of my bed nauseated by fear. In a flurry of drunken confusion, I could not, for the life of me, tell who was up to all of this. I wondered if I was doing it to myself; if the knocks and noises were just my imagination. But Maeve had heard them too. For a moment I was even convinced Maeve was responsible. But how could she rely on my passing by the newsstand and setting up the entire night? I lay there for half an hour sorting through the events of the night and putting my head back together.

Eventually I dragged myself from the floor to the bathroom. The room had an occasional spin to it and I braced myself against the sink. I felt sick but managed to keep from vomiting. I looked up at the dirty mirror and barely recognized myself. My hair was a jungle of dark knots and cowlicks. My face was blotched and red. Beneath the skin I could make out the clear lines of my cheekbones and eye sockets. As I stared longer I could see my own sunken skull, the skin just hanging in pocked jowls like a shroud draped over an urn.

Tired but entirely awake in fright, I wobbled out of the bathroom. I lay down in bed, my hands in tight fists against the sheets. My back and neck were aching from nervous tension. After a few minutes my thoughts drifted off to when I first came to the College. I remembered meeting Rosie and how we'd loved each other secretly. Now I knew she'd find out. I almost started to cry.

I could see Billy smiling now. How could I have done nothing to help him? That guilt was the wedge between Rosie and me. We just never had anyone else. I didn't know this was all going to come back again.

Excuses, all of it. I tried to relax by conjuring warm, safe memories and blocking out the rest. As my eyes closed I heard a faint lilt of music. As I fell into sleep, the music grew louder with some of the tune becoming discernible. The brass section came in and then went out again, leaving a lazy, breathy clarinet over drums. Riffs on the piano followed and then the whole band joined back in. The tune sounded like "Cherokee" or some other standard I couldn't quite make out.

I opened my eyes and adjusted to the darkness of the empty room. An arc of yellow light was cast across the hallway to my front door. Outside the windows, gray clouds picked quickly against a bruised brown night sky. I was extremely tired and felt vaguely removed, like my body was floating above the bed. I was half asleep but I felt something pulling from within myself. The music piped on softly. I stood up and walked towards the door. My motion was effortless and strange. I opened the door and looked out into the hallway.

As I peered out, I again saw the jack of hearts lying in front of me. It was now surrounded by hundreds of playing cards, all face up and scattered from my doorsill across the stairwell. There were balloons tied to the banister and confetti scattered across the landing. The jazz band grew louder and echoed in the open space. I could tell now the music was coming from downstairs.

As I walked onto the landing I could hear the pitches and scales of laughter. A series of shuffles and footfalls echoed up from the main floor. Across from where I stood, the door to the roof was propped wide open. I was in a complete daze and searching for a strand of concentration that would break the music, the mood, and my confusion.

Looking back now I would liken it to walking down the beach on a moonless night. I can hear the water breaking back on itself and can even see the surf cresting and drawing white on the beach. As I near the tide line and look around, the darkness overwhelms. My sense of where land ends and the water and sky begin is lost. I know where I am without details. There are only distant lights from the shore and the hurling, periodic eye of a faraway lighthouse. I look up and the stars cluster in unbelievable numbers—the thick gauze of the Milky Way stretching the sky into its sphere. That night as I waltzed across the landing, I had no idea about the place or time. I was drifting out to sea.

What I realize now is to be unsure of all that happened and follows.

As I climbed up the roof ladder that night there was something languid yet delightful about the music which now seeped through the night air. The roof was freezing and I had no idea what compelled me from my bed except some odd, tantalizing power. As I've said before, I was curious but not at all alert. And at the same time, I was wandering in a most precise manner. The clouded skies had lowered and there was a fine mist hanging in the air. I passed the spot where Maeve and I had first sat together. I closed my eyes and remembered her soft kisses.

I walked past the old water tower to the edge of the roof. I sat down on the ledge to look over Boston. The skyline was bleary and shrouded, the lights of the city smeared in like smoke stains. There was not a soul on the streets, and I figured the time was around four in the morning. I felt in my shirt pocket for cigarettes and found two cruelly bent. Searching for matches was when I first saw him.

"Hi there."

Tall and dark, he looked all of twenty-one. His face had a creamy smoothness that was almost devoid of features until he smiled and a warm crease came into his eyes and cheeks. That night, as on most nights I saw him, he was wearing a tuxedo that matched his black eyes and chiseled peak of black hair. There was something playboyish and impeccable about him—something easily likable yet discerning. I never had some sort of thing for him. That was never true. Whoever tells you that can go to hell with the both of us. You could say, though, that I was charmed right away, charmed as anyone would be.

"Do you need a light?"

Stunned, I turned from the ledge awkwardly, my feet sticking to the roof's tar paper. His voice sent a bolt through me. He slowly held out a book of matches.

"What the hell are you doing up here?" I finally asked.

"Well, the party was a bit boring."

His words seemed almost grave, as if he were the host. But something about the way he spoke was quite effortless—not at all glib or careless—but smooth and belying. Later I noticed that everything he said had a certain narcotic timing.

I should have known better. I should have lit my smoke and gotten down off the roof. But I was so worn out from the past few weeks, I didn't know what to do or what to think of him. The music, this man, and the roof all rolled across my brain as in a dream. His trim haircut and the slim, long lapels of his tux seemed throwbacks to another time, as if he were a secret agent in an old movie. For a brief moment I imagined a war was on and we had planned this rendezvous during a blackout or curfew of some kind.

He smiled and again offered the matches, which this time I took.

"Do I know you?" I asked.

"Oh, we've known each other in passing for some time, I think."

I looked down at the matches. They had a black-and-red cover. I opened the book to see if it was from the Mousetrap, but it was too dark to check the ad. He reached out his hand to take them back. Trying to be polite, I gave the matches to him. From below, the music still whispered on, and I heard the faintest hiccups of laughter carry from down the street.

"How often do you come up to the roof?" I asked nervously.

"I'm always breaking up here. The quiet and the view are what I need. School can get so frustrating. You know how that is."

He kept smiling, which calmed me. I tried to look closer at his face. His eyes were dark pools and difficult to read. His teeth came together in a perfect, glistening smile which was parenthesized by crescent dimples in each cheek. His expressions were an enigmatic combination of solemn and glowing. I had never before seen this face, yet somehow the feeling we had met previously was overwhelming. Whoever he was, he was dapper and intriguing. For four in the morning he was marvelously put together.

"So were you up here late last Friday?" I asked. "Were you the one over in that corner spooking the hell out of me?"

"Spook you? Come on now. Last week I saw you up here with that pretty girl. Both of you were three sheets to the wind and rather scared me. I was just minding my business and getting some fresh air. I did, though, feel like an intruder to your little amorous world."

I lit my cigarette. The band was playing an old Charlie Parker number. "Do you live in Adams?"

"I did once. I must say that if this party is any indication, it's not as fun as it once was. Could I have one of those?"

A part of me was confused why I was still talking with him. The other part was trying to recall where I might have known him from. I handed him the other crumpled cigarette and gave him a slight apologetic look. "All I have."

"Say, where's that girlfriend of yours tonight? The one with the short black dress."

I thought of Rosie and lowered my head in guilt. "She's not my girlfriend, and I think you scared her off."

"Not your girlfriend? But you two seem meant for each

other. Although it's hard to find, I know true love when I see it." His smile was turning into an arrogant thing.

"Pardon me, but you don't know what you're talking about."

"Oh, don't get upset. She just reminded me of a close lady friend I once had. We would hang out here on cool, moonlit nights, drinking and singing together." For the first time he seemed to trail off and look away from me. "So if she's not your girlfriend, who is this mysterious woman?"

I should have asked myself the same question. Instead I got up from the ledge and stood straight with him. "None of your business, really."

At this he laughed and turned toward the ledge. He gazed over at downtown Boston. "I guess I know her as well as you do, then."

"Yeah, she talks about you all the time." I wanted to walk away, but I was compelled by earlier suspicions. "Who are you?"

"How do you really know someone?" He dropped his cigarette, sighed out his last puff of smoke like a sleepy dragon, and tapped the butt out with the sole of his loafer. "Or even yourself?"

It was a cold night, but as he spoke no frost came from his mouth. A fright rose in me suddenly. Behind him, the lights of the skyline winked silently. I backed away, taking slow, casual steps. I tried to play it cool. "One of the great questions, professor, and one too late in the night or early in the morning to answer."

I smiled at him. He returned with a sly look that feigned indifference. "Not one now to mock your own grinning?" he said.

"What?"

"What about your thesis? How's that going?" The music had stopped. "Your passion ending, your purpose lost."

I smiled again, pretending to comprehend. "Time to go."

He turned and stepped between me and the roof door. I tried to make my way past him, but he clutched me by the wrists. His eyes, now catching the lurid glow of the streetlights, bored into the back of my head. I tried to pull back, but he drew closer, and I felt a cold sweat crawl down my neck. I lost my vision while trying to step back toward the ledge. A series of buzzing circles came across my eyes and fractured into a field of misfired rods and cones. Then utter darkness. I was blind, helpless.

"You don't know a thing," he said with a voice hollow and pained. "Grief and despair are taught in this life. My fury is yours."

The bells of St. Paul's stirring me, I woke on the rooftop the next morning.

That afternoon I staggered towards Lamont library in an attempt to shore the ruins of my academic career. Before leaving B-entry, I went down to my room and played the one message that was blinking on my machine. It was my thesis adviser. The department (i.e., his wonderful self) had looked over my last-minute rewrite of the outline and sample chapter.

"The analysis, not to mention the writing and grammar, was threadbare, and you didn't account for the histories. I need to talk to you sometime this week about forgoing the rest of senior tutorial . . ."

I slammed my fist down on the answering machine. Pompous asshole—didn't have the guts to tell me in person. And why would he have read it so fast unless he had been planning to reject me all along.

So it was official now—I was a complete fuckup. What

was left to do that I hadn't failed at or been asked to forgo? I had even quit my internship at the magazine to concentrate on the thesis. I think they were glad to see me take off. All I was ever good at was jamming the Xerox machine. My overly hectic schedule had been reduced to a midday hangover. The news about the thesis was too much to handle. I wouldn't graduate with honors. More important, I wouldn't have a chance to prove them wrong. In the eyes of the department, I wasn't even worth the opportunity.

By the time I had come to my senses the afternoon sun was already bloodshot and done. I tottered along the south side of the Yard trying to avoid the arctic blasts of wind that ravined through the buildings. I was sick with myself and almost thankful for being rid of my thesis and adviser. The whole enterprise had become an esoteric, self-perpetuating contest that came down to critics humping critics.

I hobbled along, upset by all of this. The early-evening sky met the ground in a purple that bled to gray. I was heading to the library to take a whack at all the work from my normal classes that had been put on hold by the Marshall and the thesis. The red brick buildings of the old Yard crouched and sank low to the narrow paths cutting through them. I had several papers on extension but I hadn't cracked a book for any of them. Utterly exhausted and confused from the long night, I was also running a slight fever from sleeping in the cold air. The previous night had spun me into an extended daze that I tried to trudge past and forget. The seeds of my memory were scattered. My entire body tensed up to the harsh winds. It was too cold to think things over.

I walked through two sets of doors and into Lamont

Library. As I passed through the first-floor reference section, I noticed a stack of freshman facebooks along the wall. I stopped and opened the one for my class. Flipping through the facebooks was an important pastime at the College. Name, parents' address, and prep school—what else did we really need to know?—a repetitive list of landed gentry and the children of professors.

Page by page, I searched for my mysterious roof companion. I was uncertain where to start and soon the headshots were pixeling into one smiling caricature of an incoming freshman. He said he had once lived in Adams. Trying hard to focus, I was barely able to remember what he actually looked like. It was dark, I was very drunk, and despite my having seen his face straight on, my memory flickered and waned. The more I attempted to picture him, the less I could recall. Nonetheless, I scrutinized the facebooks, determined to pick him out of a lineup.

For over an hour, I went through four facebooks and spotted no semblance of him. He acted as if he went to the College, but maybe he had transferred in as a sophomore. Until that semester, I was fairly sure I had never seen him in lecture or the dining hall.

The more I searched for his face the more it disappeared from my mind. All the process left me with was a piercing headache. Since the moment I'd woken up on the roof, I had been painfully embarrassed to have passed out on this utter stranger. I was fearful and paranoid to begin with, but the events of the previous night were creepy to the point of unreal. I was not going to dismiss our encounter, though. A deep, nascent part of me had a sense that I would see him again.

When I put down the facebooks my eyes met with Rosie's as she was walking out of the main reading room. She looked stressed out, but arguably happy to have run into me. Had she lost weight since I last noticed? Regardless, the charcoal circles around her eyes told the story. I apologized up and down for not being around much since her return from New York. That launched her into a lecture.

"I'm very easy to deal with. I know you are going through a tough time, but so am I. Just tell me what you want to do and we'll make separate plans. It's that simple and I don't ask for much."

I swallowed these remarks with an uneasy silence due in part to the suffocating feeling they produced in me. All we had, sadly, was each other. I did miss her and something lately had stirred up those earlier times. She could be mean, but she could also be tender. Each time I was exhausted by her rants and critiques of my life, I thought about the short, wild love we had, and I just couldn't break it off. I needed her somehow and I saw the same in her tired eyes.

Still, our recent distancing had been more than gradual and I couldn't bring myself to tell her about my thesis. So after a few blank moments, I politely responded, "It's not that I don't want to be with you. I just feel pulled in so many ways by my work and friends. I just need some space and time."

"You look like hell."

"I feel like hell. I'm sorry." There was an awkward pause.

"What are we doing for Halloween?"

Halloween fell on the following Saturday. It was one of the best weekends on campus because midterms were finally over and all sorts of parties were happening. Adams House cleared out the dining hall and threw a masquerave. In the midst of avoiding Rosie and my life, I had forgotten that I was hosting the fourth floor of B-entry's Heaven and Hell.

Heaven and Hell was the customary pre-party to the rave. Excluding the main floor, the entry was set up in the three Dantesque categories—Hell on the second floor, Purgatory on third, and Heaven on the fourth. The fourth floor and my room had recently seemed more of a desperate and damned circle in the divine comedy. But by the time All Hallows' Eve rolled around, the top of Adams B had taken on a paradisal transformation, with ungodly amounts of alcohol flowing from its pearly gates. The juniors across the hall from me stuck cotton clouds all over the landing, angel wings on the doorways, and blue gels over the lights. A few hours before the party, I tried to open the roof to Heaven, but found the hasp had been replaced since that last night I was there.

For Halloween, I went as Cary Grant in *North by Northwest*, wearing a blue serge suit, a gray tie, and sunglasses. Rosie, whose roommates were sponsoring Hell, dressed up as a vampire witch from an Anne Rice novel.

Heaven was quickly stormed by partygoers. Around ten, the dry ice had melted and Michael made his way up from Limbo. I pulled him aside and together we did five boilermakers in a quarter of an hour—a new record worth celebrating at the rave.

Michael had a glazed, happy look in his eye, but it was yet to be determined whether he'd be able to stay standing. "So where's Maeve?" he asked.

"Keep it down. Rosie might be lurking around the corner," I said.

"She's really nice," he slurred with a devilish grin.

"Okay, you need to hold off." I too was feeling the whiskeys on top of beers on top of whiskeys. We were leaning against my door on the fourth-floor landing, but I for one was starting to feel the tilt of the earth's axis. The crowd was buzzing. Their faces had a weird glow in the blue light. The tinting brought out the shadows and whites of everyone's eyes and mouth, exaggerating both the angelic and diabolical.

Michael took a step into my room and held himself against the wall of the hallway. He looked close to passing out, and I asked if he was all right.

"Yeah, can I just stay in here for a minute or two?"

"Sure, but I have to go to Rosie's room and take her down to the rave." It didn't look like Michael cared much about my whereabouts as he crawled across my room to the bed. But then as I turned from him, he called to me.

"I just want to let you know that I'll be down in a minute." I waved goodbye, as he sat upright on the bed. At that moment, Michael looked completely sober. "I just need to rest for a second and then I'll follow you down. Forget what I said about Rosie."

I left my room a bit puzzled by his act. He hadn't said anything about Rosie. But maybe what he was saying about Maeve was meant to be about Rosie. Lord knows. He was gone, and as I made my way through the crowd for Heaven, I realized Michael had been under a lot of the same pressures as me. Drunk talk was drunk talk, and at the time I didn't have too many wits about me to give it much thought. So I went downstairs and dragged Rosie to the rave. I was so stewed, she seriously asked me if someone had spilt their drink on me. By the time I got her to the edge of the dance floor she would have nothing to do with me. Instead she ran off to a corner to be mollified by her girlfriends. I was too drunk to notice and made my way across the floor to Michael, who had come downstairs and appeared to be in great shape. We danced with a few of his friends from Tufts. The music was loud enough to induce a heart murmur and the lights were on full strobe. A bizarre and ghoulish transcendence occurred as I surveyed the throng of costumed ravers in the brief blinks of light. Everyone was wearing a mask and there was something nightmarish and unnerving about recognizing so few of the people around me. But I let that fear pass and soon I was thrashing about, getting lost among the hundreds of people sardined onto the dance floor. The place felt like an oven and you could see jets of steam and smoke making their way out the back windows.

Just as the beat dropped to pick up a new track, I spotted him. He was back and away from the dance floor, sitting alone on a windowsill, dressed in a black cloak. His face was partly masked, and it took me several long looks before I was convinced it was him. My first thought was to ignore him. I wondered why he was by himself. Then I wanted to follow him. I craned my neck around a group of the raving undead and found him staring straight at me.

I pretended not to notice and danced around to where I thought I could observe him undetected. I cut around two Siamese blondes stitched together in a giant pair of overalls. I took my sunglasses from my jacket pocket and put them on. When I looked again, it was just in time to see him leaving the windowsill and hopping down into the adjacent courtyard. He turned left and I watched through the other window in his path. I didn't see him pass.

I stopped dancing as this happened and a few moments later pulled my way through the crowd to the window. As nonchalantly as possible, I put a hand to the window frame and peeked through. A few steps away, he popped around the corner. I startled back and he began to laugh. His laugh was washed out by the music and all I could see was his face and mouth, which seemed to spasm hideously out of control. His eyes and forehead were covered by a skull mask, His long, white teeth fanged and glistened from beneath the mask catching the dim light of the courtyard.

As quickly as he had emerged from behind the corner, he was gone again. Astonished for a moment, I jumped over the windowsill and into the courtyard. Toward the far wall I saw him again, by himself and from behind. His black coat had merged into the shadows and cigarette smoke wafted from the edge of his mask. He had been following me. I was sure of it. And now I had trapped him. With each step I was getting more and more angry that this jackass had been stalking me. I wanted an explanation. A step away, I grabbed him by the shoulder and jerked him around.

And there was Maeve wrapped in a black shawl. She had on lots of dark eyeliner and her hair was streaked white. She looked scary and cute, like a disheveled Fury.

"What the hell."

"I thought you were this guy who's been creeping me out." I pulled off my sunglasses to look her in the eye.

"What?"

"I'm sorry. I thought you were someone else." We were both screaming over the music. "I tied one on earlier with Michael and I think I'm starting to see things."

"You drink more than you sleep." She was wearing torn fishnets that now peeked from below her coat. "You look like hell."

"People keep saying."

"I had fun the other night." She stubbed out her cigarette and then looked straight at me with those darling, wet eyes. "I'm sorry I sort of ran out of there, but that girlfriend of yours scared me to death."

My eyes quickly darted around to see if Rosie was nearby. "I know, I had fun too, and I'm sorry that spoiled it."

Maeve gave me a mischievous smile. "Do you want to get out of here? We could go by the station. There's a mellower party over there."

Something about it sounded ill-fated to me, but how could I let her go? I put my two fingers close to her lips, grasping an imaginary joint. "Do you mean what I think you mean?"

"Perhaps."

In addition to being beautiful and smart, Maeve was a subrock DJ at the campus radio station. The radioheads at the College were generally a bunch of freaks—imagine Dr. Demento's target audience on psychedelics. And there were more people working and hanging out at the station than actually listened to it. Many believed the station's wattage was in the oversized lightbulb category because of all the heat lighting in the basement.

Maeve and I crossed Mass Ave into the Yard. It was freezing cold, and I could feel the mild fever which had plagued me most of the week break up in it. Wearing only my blue suit, I was thoroughly frozen, except for the hand which held Maeve's. We passed several other costumed couples—Fred and Ginger, Marilyn and Joe D., Marilyn and JFK, Wonder Woman and Superman—on our way. The Yard was calm except for the trees scratching in the wind. In the corner of my eye I saw someone moving in the shadows behind Emerson Hall. It could have been him, and I was unsettled by it. Maeve noticed I was getting anxious, kissed me on the cheek, and tried to smile it off.

I forced a grin back and we headed into the radio station, housed in the basement of Memorial Hall. From the moment we entered, I could tell these wonks were freaked out of their collective acid jazz mind. At the time I didn't know what ether smelled like, but the place was rank. Maeve and I shared unsure looks. Her friend Jeremy came running to greet us.

"Frank is in the control room just freaking. He's barred the door and has been playing Ornette Coleman's 'Lonely Woman' for four hours straight. He stops every once in a while to drop, chew on the DATs, or shout obscenities about his father—" There was a muted crash in the direction of the control room. Jeremy kept going, "—who apparently has a thing for his sister."

Maeve looked at Jeremy for a while with heavy, indolent eyes, then shifted over to me.

"I love Ornette Coleman."

We both laughed.

Then we looked for drugs.

Jeremy eventually found us a few shrooms. I later

learned that he didn't have a clue who I was and thought I was one of Maeve's friends from New York. Maeve and I shared a last slice of pizza to eat the shrooms with. We then drank eight glasses of water between us to sober up and hydrate.

Within twenty minutes, the hallway began to fold like mirrors in a pattern of infinite recession. The off-white walls of the station flickered orange, then red. Maeve was also coming on-line when Frank blew out all the lights from the control room. The darkness came glimmering and soft like crushed velvet and I lifted my hand to push into the void. Maeve was struggling to light a cigarette. The room breathed.

I looked around the radio station. Hadn't Billy done radio freshman year? It seemed so long ago. No, I shouldn't think about that now, especially now. I tried to play it cool in front of Maeve, but the mirages were coming on strong. I looked down at the floor and concentrated. Regardless, the seams in the tiles started to bend and kaleidoscope out of shape.

Then I remembered what was below the floor. Billy had shown it to me that one time I was not going to think about. There was a door in Matthews that led down there. Maeve and I needed a change of venue. Maybe he just told me one time, or I read about it. I smiled at Maeve. It would be a good place for this.

"How are we going to break in?"

"The radio station has a key. That's where the cable to the antenna runs."

Maeve looked unsure, but I compelled her to look for the key. I was soaring at that point, the best I ever felt. Maybe we shouldn't head for the tunnels, I thought, things were fine up here. Besides, where would we go?

It took what seemed like hours to find the key. Maeve was all sorts of warm colors now. I had to kiss her again, and that's what ultimately urged me to take her down there. We made for the tunnel entrance. We passed Jeremy trying to entice Frank out of his bunker with hash brownies. We reached the door and Maeve had no problem unlocking it. I took one last look around the station. I felt uneasy, like we were being watched. No, it was the drugs bending the corners.

The old steam tunnels ran under the entire campus, and were an ideal place to trip. These older tunnels were used mostly now for computer and radio wiring. Portions of the tunnels were completely dark, but the entrances and exits were lit and well marked. The main sections were wide enough to stand up in with a slight bend. The air was very dank because the new steam tunnels ran right below them, about six inches away. You could feel the heat coming off the floor and the moisture sweating and trickling down from the top. Surges of hot water trembled through the joints and discharge pipes below, creating a low constant thunder in the older tunnel.

Maeve and I could barely walk but we made our way steadily past the art museum and the eastern half of the Yard. We then came upon a section of tunnel that after a couple turns around the foundation of the library opened onto a small alcove where we could both stand straight up. I stopped Maeve there and took her hand. We were both panting for breath in the thick, moist air.

"Where are we?" she asked. Even in the tunnel's dimness, her eyes caught the light like diamonds.

"We have to work on your paper, so I brought you to Widener." Then I stooped forward and kissed her. Her warm breath rushed through me.

We kissed and groped for some time, each touch taking us deeper into some dark chemical strangeness. My head began to spin with lust and excitement. My hands were moving south at a good steady pace when Maeve pulled away complaining of stomach pain. I didn't want to lose our romantic momentum, so I suggested we push on to where the tunnels crossed Mass Ave and then on to Adams House and my room.

I was surprised at how quickly we went—the tunnels

must have run downhill slightly. The dark, narrow way felt like walking through a dream. It was all nebulously familiar. My déjà vu was really baffled by the drugs. Their combined effect hit me in strange waves of anticipation and nostalgia.

Upon reaching Mass Ave, the tunnels narrowed to a crawl space above the subway. At this point, the new steam pipe ran alongside the old, disused one. The rush of steam was at a much higher pitch as it was forced through a smaller channel. The airflow in this portion whistled by like a jet. The shrooms were laying sear marks on my brain as Maeve and I sat exhausted next to this giant underground teakettle.

Out of breath and unable to keep things in any sort of check, I suggested we find Adams as quickly as possible. Maeve agreed things were too heavy. I was fairly sure which subtunnel led to Adams, but we had to go through the crawl space. I went first and tried hard not to hallucinate any foot-long rats waiting to peck out my eyes. I wriggled on my belly to the other end and then tried to yank Maeve through. After several pulls and a lift, we were both standing again at the other end of the crawl space.

We headed left, still guessing the way back to Adams. The tunnels at this point were full of shunts and run-offs, and the condensation had thickened to a mist. I was worried but promised Maeve that I knew where we were going. It was then that I looked down at her arm and found it covered in blood. I freaked completely and then realized it was only sweat and steam blotting her clothes.

"I've got to get us out of here." I was stupidly crying—a side effect I had experienced before and was unable to control. "This is too creepy. Let's go, before I lose it."

"Keep your shit together. Fucking lightweight."

I looked up in stunned silence at her. I tried to find the whites in Maeve's eyes but just saw these gleaming black irises. Her outburst reminded me of someone else, but then she came around. "Darling, I was talking to myself. Sorry. Let's go. The door is down here, right?"

Another fifty feet and we're at a door marked A-HOUSE. A good sign, and Maeve tried the key. She jiggled it a few times.

"Shit. I think this lock is rusted shut."

"Let me try."

All of a sudden everything came down to super slow motion. I was playing with the lock and looking at Maeve. The hissing steam filled my ears with its insidious static. The noise tore the patience out of me. I remembered freshman year. I was crying hysterically. This is how I got out of Matthews. I banged against the door, yelling furiously. What was I running from? I tried to grab the key and shove the door open. This was where I hid. I was drunk. Had Billy been with me?

The key broke in the lock. Nothing bad had happened.

Maeve stopped for a second and then slumped away from the door and into the tunnel. It was at this point that things took on a weird life of their own.

"What the fuck's the matter with you?" she hissed.

"You're just too far gone to deal with any of this," I was very angry and confused.

"You moron, you're the one who broke the key in the goddam door."

"Go fuck yourself."

"Why not. It'd be better than you."

At that, Maeve started heading back into the tunnel. Between the steam and the hallucinations she was gone from my sight almost instantly. I should have helped Billy, but there was a knock at the door, and I got scared. I called to her a couple times but the dampness made my voice fall like a whisper. I suddenly realized how far the walk back to the station was. I was still crying, and wasn't certain if it was a side effect anymore. This was all Rosie's fault. She must have told Billy about us. I tried to look ahead through the tunnel but my vision just shifted and blurred into vaporous clouds.

I leaned back against the door and suddenly the latch clicked open and I fell through.

"Christ. Maeve!"

But she had gone off. I was alone and terrified. Why was she angry? I was the one with the right to be angry. I had fought so hard to keep that night out of my mind. I had tried to stay level-headed. But here amid these underground surges and rumbles, it all came back with unbridled shame.

And then I sensed someone watching me. Deep inside me, guilt churned and mulled. And now that basest of fears came racing up my spine. And I knew who it would be. The entire trip through the tunnels had become a disaster. I had to stop this dream. I had to wake up and get out there. But someone was watching.

I turned and looked through the doorway. And there, behind the open door, I saw Billy.

I was on my hands and knees, and he stood above me. I was arrested in fright, tears streaming down to my chin. I tried to look away—think of something else, anything—but my gaze was fixed on him. His broad chest and arms were as strong and muscular as I remembered, and I trembled at how vivid his presence seemed. His lower body and legs sank into the gloom behind the door. Look away, I told myself, he's not really there. His face was gaunt, ashen, devoid of emotion. His eyes, like a cat's, only reflected the dim light of the tunnel. He was like a statue—perfect, distant, and still. Then he outstretched his hand to me.

No. I was doing this. It was the drugs and I was allowing them to get to me. This was my fear, not Billy's. But his hand, his arm, seemed so real. I began to reach out to touch him. Was he smiling as I did this? I stretched out a little farther. That's when I saw the hideous scar around his neck and I remembered what had happened between us. I should have helped him, but I couldn't. I lurched back, pressing myself against the doorway. Still he looked at me—cautious, serene—like he was reaching out to a frightened animal.

This had to stop. I looked away, trying to snap out of this tortured illusion. My throat clenched tightly and my breathing staggered over a few dry coughs. I could feel the tears welling and then falling from the bottom rims of my eyes. Don't look. Don't be so afraid. Look away. Look away from him. But I could hear him asking. The same questions I had asked myself a thousand times. Why? Why didn't you help me? Why didn't you tell me? Why was her watch on your dresser? Her hairs on your pillow? Why did you tell them you went away for the weekend? You could have stopped me. Why? Why me? Why did you betray me? Things rank and gross. We could have been happy. The two of us. Rosie and I. You and I.

"I loved too," I cried, but went unheard. The doorway was empty. No trace of Billy. No one was watching me. I was alone. Was it me? No trace, except for my dreaded memory of him.

I had to find Maeve and get out of that place. I picked

up my senses from the floor of the doorway and ran after her. She must have been running too, because I only caught up with her back at the crawl space. I peered through the opening but had trouble seeing her. My eyes blacked out for a few seconds. In this momentary darkness I cried out, "Maeve, the door opened. Come back."

My vision then jacked up into a blue screen. I was growing more and more impatient and felt like a busted TV. The blue field turned red, then a hazy brown. These mushrooms were way too sick. I blinked myself into focus and found Maeve turning herself around in the crawlspace.

I lost my balance and fell back. I saw Maeve looking at me.

"There's somebody on the other side of this thing," she said.

"You're looking at me."

"But I see someone else."

"You're fucked up. Come this way."

"I'm scared."

A small recessed circle began to open in the crawl space. I lost 3D for a moment and Maeve, the tunnel and all space flattened into me. I stepped back trying to judge distance again.

The shunt in the side of the crawl space was completely open now. Maeve yelled for help. Again things were falling apart in a peaceful slow motion. I had stepped forward trying to drag her out of the crawl space when I twitched into clarity and ducked away. I was trying to help, help them both. My head felt like a bubble ready to burst. A red light started to blink from below the open side of the tunnel. Ten yards behind me a door at the end of the tunnel section began to fall from the ceiling. I could hear the gears of the door wrenching down. That noise was soon replaced by a blood-curdling wail as water turning to air ran behind the walls alongside me.

I ran back towards the falling door. The door was thick, metallic, and wet and wouldn't stop under my hands. A desperate fear gushed through me. I slid under the door to the other side. The wail of the pipes rose in pitch to a violent shriek. The whole tunnel began to tremble.

Maeve screamed my name as the door slammed down. I staggered back from the section. The steam off the rusty pipes stung my eyes. I was wrapped in delusion and could barely breathe. The door bent into a whine as the crawl space filled instantly with jets of steam. A series of low thuds bellowed from the crawl-space side of the door. The thuds turned into a methodical pounding and the pressure in the section surged back and forth. I felt intense heat coming off the door, which at that point I was more than ten feet away from. Then the pounding stopped.

The rushing steam quieted to a slow, dying whistle.

I reeled out of the tunnels into the Adams House basement. A fever raked and flared over me like coals spitting from scratched-out ashes. I blindly staggered along a narrow corridor rank with decay and rat droppings. I came to a flight of stairs, clutched the balustrade, tottered to the side, and vomited. Every inch of my insides pounded forward into my chest. I tried in vain to regain composure at the foot of the stairs. Within my head, the sound of steam whistled incessantly. My heart was racing and a combination of sweat and steam had soaked through my entire suit. I looked up the stairs. The basement windows were filled with a predawn purple hue. I gathered my strength into climbing the stairs and ended up in a hallway a few doors down from B-entry. I hobbled toward the main floor.

Purging my stomach had cleared my head enough for

me to take the first flight of stairs rather quickly. As I reached the second flight I lost my balance and fell to the landing. A sharp pain shot across my head and I felt an enormous weight pulling back on me as if I were dragging my own body up the stairs. The hallway began to sway and the grimy detritus of Hell's party—plastic cups, cigarette butts, bottles, and streamers—tumbled from one side of the landing to the other. I pulled myself up two more steps. My vision of the second floor faded out for a few minutes. As if I were suffering from the bends, I could feel the air pressure behind my eyes. My blindness resolved into an image of Maeve being boiled alive, her body and blood superheated into a thick, red cloud.

I swallowed a scream and dragged myself along the railing. An ice-cold draft seeped across the stairwell. I climbed to the third floor. I could hear faint, hollow tricklings of music and laughter carry down the hall. The slightest noise reverberated endlessly to the point I couldn't tell what was echoing in my head and what I was actually hearing. I reached the fourth floor and the music was replaced with a desperate pounding. I looked across the landing and saw Maeve covered in blood hammering at my door. She was screaming but no sound came forth except the pounding. Horrified, I looked away, but her knocking persisted and I was afraid someone would come into the hall and spot us. I lunged across the landing to stop her, only to slam into my own door headfirst. The pounding trailed off down the stairs and fell into rhythm with the syncopated limp of my own heart.

I turned the doorknob and fell into my room. Behind me thick coils of steam were making their way up the stairs. The steam coalesced into a growing cloud of hisses and wails, carrying the streamers and silvery glitter of

Heaven along with it. The cloud rose up and quickly covered the landing. Its movement was hypnotic—its dark billows climbing and falling over each other. A gray tendril of steam shot forward. The menacing cloud had suddenly grown to within a few feet of me, and I kicked the door closed. The force of the steam hitting the door violently rattled the lock and hinges.

After a few moments, the rattling ceased. The hallway was silent. Water dripped down the door and began to pool on the floor. I lay nearly paralyzed with dread. The smell from the steam had a sickening, ammonia quality that singed my nostrils.

After several minutes, I turned into my room convinced that the shrooms had driven me completely out of my mind. I was weak with fright and just wanted to sleep. I struggled across my room trying to remember what was real and what imagined. I remembered the party. The Heaven and Hell party, the rave, and following him across the courtyard came swelling back into memory. The French doors to my room shook with the wind.

At that point I was spun around by a tremendous feeling that my life had fallen into the pages of a story and that truth was no longer conceivable. My room, the hallway, my bed, my clothes became instruments in accompaniment. The noise was gaining harmony. It was all emphatic and clear. As suddenly as it had risen, the music had faded, the laughter died. My hands were covered in what I knew was Maeve's blood. These hands that held her with some hope of escape or at least happy defeat. I fell on my bed babbling her name as if I could resurrect her. Before morning came, I fell into tormented sleep.

I woke up later that morning to an alarm clock I didn't remember setting. I sat up in bed. The blood drained out of my head, leaving a blunt, throbbing agony. I turned over onto my back and tried to open my eyes, which were blurred with sleep. I stared for a moment at the light peeking through the shades. The windows and walls gradually came into focus. The room was silent and gloomy. My headache was terrible and I could barely sit up in the bed. I reached into the jacket I was still wearing from the night before in search of a cigarette. As I brought my hand back I found it covered in blood. I blanched with fear and jumped out of the bed. The sheets were covered in blood. The bedframe and radiator were smeared with blood. My room looked like an abattoir. The amount of blood was sickening. I felt strangely removed from myself as I looked down at the bed. It was like looking at my own murder.

I heard voices in the hall outside my door. Suddenly the whole night and Maeve's death swarmed into memory. I stripped the bedsheets and took off my clothes. Removing my shirt, I realized I had cut my wrist and arm badly and all this blood could well be my own. I gagged as its curdled rankness came into my nostrils. I felt faint and wanted to fall back to the bed. But I held myself steady against the dresser and bundled my clothes with the sheets and tried to take them into the bathroom. The bathroom door was stuck. I heard footsteps approaching in the hallway. I froze. But the person turned and entered the room next door. My suspicions grew wildly and I decided to burn the sheets and clothes in the fireplace. With all this blood, cleaning things in the bathtub would have taken hours. I needed to burn everything—destroy the sheets, my clothes, and throw away the ashes. I didn't know what had happened, but the one thing I did know was that I couldn't get caught like this. I put on jeans and a T-shirt and begin to mop the blood from the mattress and floor. I couldn't believe what I was doing. I was both disgusted and amazed at the amount of blood that must have flowed from my wrist. I found some bleach in the closet. It had to be my wrist. I wadded the sheets and my clothes into a ball. Then with the bleach I washed down the bedposts, the radiator, and the floor.

I opened the flue to the fireplace and tore up a few old paperbacks for kindling. I sprinkled lighter fluid on them, heated the air in the flue, and then slowly moved the bedsheets over the fire. I remembered seeing him at the dance and then mistaking Maeve for him later. The fire torched up but then died out quickly without catching.

There were more footsteps in the hallway. I tried to remember who had last seen me with Maeve. For over an hour I poured lighter fluid onto the hearth until every inch of paper and sheet had been burnt into ash.

As the fire died down, I tried to picture Maeve's face as I'd seen it for the last time. But what had happened? I had no sense whatsoever and was terribly upset and frustrated for remembering so little. I was desperate and afraid. I recalled the tunnel but couldn't account for that section closing off. I knew that the steam tunnels had runoffs and shunts, but that crawl space was a thinned-out section over subway lines and wiring. The area was a bottleneck in the system. It wasn't a place to reroute.

But it was a place to cut the steam off. It was so dark and hellish down there. The fire blazed up unexpectedly, catching on some synthetic fiber in the clothes. I lurched back and prepared to douse the fireplace, then the flame diminished on its own. Why had we ever gone in?

Then I remembered that Maeve had said there was someone else there.

I couldn't swallow my fears. My body was a tension wire. I just wanted to hide and not face any of this. What if I came forward, I thought. I could clear my name, but hours had passed and that would seem like I was holding out. The police could find him better than I could. The truth could be told. I hadn't done anything besides cheat on Rosie and I didn't even have to admit that.

No, my story made no sense. I had no witnesses. What if they gave me a drug test? I was the only one there and all this blood traced events back to me. They would certainly find some part of me—a hair or something—on her body. They wouldn't believe my crazy, shroom-addled story. No. I had to hold back and lie low. I had to withdraw and piece things together for myself. I slapped at my head with the palm of my hand, struggling to remember. In between the spaces of my memory was a sense that the truth could only be told by Maeve, who would soon be noticed as missing. And I was last seen with.

My paranoia grew from this and I could feel him almost cheering it on. I knew he was watching me all that night. He must have been lurking behind us in those tunnels. It made no sense and it was the only sense I could make.

If he, not I, murdered Maeve, the rest fell into place. Too many things had happened by accident. Too many doors being tried and corners whisked around. I had been in a near-deliberate daze for weeks and I was beginning to understand why. The music from the rooftop, my forgetting his face—details and lack of details, proof and no proof. All that it left was the blood on my hands.

I patted out the remaining cinders in the fireplace and decided to leave my room. I looked over at the closet, its contents still strewn at the bottom. It irked me to think that he might have been in the room at some point. His lingering presence there sent chills through me and I couldn't think straight as a result. I put on my coat and baseball cap and darted down the stairs out of B-entry.

I walked out onto Mass Ave. It was an overcast day just past noon that already felt like early evening. I felt sick to my stomach and walked up Mass Ave glaring at passersby. Everybody was so carefree and idle. Despite the clouds and the rain, the streets around the Square were filled with tourists and shoppers. I despised their business—everyone so blithe and insouciant. I felt ashamed by their freedom. From that Halloween night on, I was yoked to Maeve's death for all time. I glanced down at my fingernails, which were still lined with the faintest traces of dried blood. I looked again at the rush of people glistening from the recent rain. I resented them all. I passed the newsstand in the Square, where thoughts of Maeve shuddered through me again. I loathed myself for getting trapped. I was so afraid. My eyes darted over the *Globe* and the College paper but I saw no headlines about Maeve's disappearance. It was too soon.

I turned onto Brattle Street. I kept my head down, my eyes hiding below the bill of my cap. I tried to think clearly. Just as Maeve came into the picture so did he. Why was Rosie dead set on berating me? Why had Michael acted so strange last night? Who could I count on? Who else knew this had happened? Maeve's death could be another door opening and shutting, another trick being played on me. I crossed the street forgetting to look for cars. A blue sedan came within inches of hitting me. The car's horn blared away until it blended back into the Cambridge traffic.

I was certain the steam blow had killed her, but then again I hadn't seen her die.

She came on so strong even though she knew about Rosie and me. No, the rest of that thinking failed—Maeve was kind and wonderful and I was being selfish and depraved.

I walked down Brattle until I reached Mount Auburn Cemetery. Past the gates and rows of the recently buried I pushed on, deeper into the older part of the cemetery. A cold wind blasted across the open field of endless headstones. I reached a dark obelisk commemorating the Union dead. From there I followed a yew-lined path to the left. The path brought me alongside a dell where a small pond was showing the first signs of freezing. The ice spread against the pond in white spines. The trail then rose over a small hill and passed the grave of Winslow Homer. I crossed over to a series of ponds and watched flocks of Canada geese take off and land. I sat on a stone bench there for quite some time, trying to calm down, trying to think. In this part of the cemetery a losing battle was being fought between the landscaping and the briers. Gravestones lining the ponds were overgrown and falling into the hedgerows. The ground rose and beveled softly and I could picture where the bones and skulls of the deceased had dwindled into dirt. Creeper vines held the winding paths like so many delicate fingers. Marble-trunked maples rattled off the last of their leaves to the wind.

Below where I sat were a series of ancient family crypts dug into a hill that sloped down to the ponds. Each crypt housed the dead forebears of old Brahmin clans—Cabot, Lowell, Thayer, Longfellow, Weld, and other familiar Pilgrim names.

I had never been so close to death as I was with Maeve's murder. And I knew it was murder and I was right all along to be paranoid. I was being set up.

Right—they hide in the tunnels and hunker on rooftops. There were no hidden meanings. No one cared enough to do all of this to me. My muddled thoughts were my own worst nightmare. I tried to avoid self-pity and focus on events as they had happened.

I wandered down to the crypts and peeked through holes left by the intricate carvings in the crypt doors. I stopped at the Adams crypt and allowed my eyes to adjust to the darkness within. The air was cold and still. A bust of a small boy came into view and eerily stared back at me. I tried to imagine what sickness or accident had caused his death. Dried roses, shriveled and black like frostbitten arms, were draped on the doors of individual tombs. All these conflicts and joys now silent in their graves. I let out a breath and the mist carried into the room and hung like smoke.

Watching my own breath pass over the walls of the crypt, I realized something very important. It came to me quickly and I almost lost the thought in its passing. I understood that Maeve had surely died and what that meant for my life. I was also certain that he too was dead, and was yielding some strange but real power over me. I felt tricked and trapped into this world of the dead. The shame, the guilt, of Billy's death, and now this. It was getting dark. The afternoon shadows had long since fallen over the crypt doors. I quietly vowed to myself that whatever it took I had to survive the oncoming winter.

I walked back towards Adams House. The day's grayness had darkened into evening. The streetlamps had come on, but their shine was useless in the twilight. I traipsed past the old Colonial houses on Brattle, their shutters sagging from the windows like the sad, painted eyes of clowns. Turning into B-entry, I half expected the police to be waiting for me. They weren't. Instead I found Rosie's roommate Susan hanging out on the landing of the second floor.

"Where have you been?"

"The cemetery, digging my own grave for midterms," I said.

"You look like you were disinterred." Susan was friendly enough when it suited her. At that very moment, though, she wanted to finish her card game rather than be sympathetic to me. She laid out a row of cards. "Where have you been this year? I rarely see you."

"I don't know, here and there. Trying to figure out what to do," I said.

"Me too. I can't wait for this semester to be over."

"Amen." I smiled thoughtlessly, just waiting to get past this conversation.

Susan, however, had taken an interest in me. She kept looking me over, trying to figure out why I was so spaced out. "You want something to drink?" she said, pointing to some bottles of a Mexican beer.

I took one while Susan proceeded to shuffle her deck of cards. "Solitaire?" I asked.

"No, I'm reading my fortune."

"Fascinating science." I slunk against the wall, taking pains to squeeze a lime wedge through the neck of my beer bottle. Susan was sitting on the floor. She shifted her weight and began a three-card reading—past, present, and future—for herself. She looked unhappy at what she foresaw, and her dismay tempted me to act out my suspicions.

"Why don't you do a reading for Adams House?" I suggested

"You have to ask the cards a question."

"Well then, how about: is B-entry haunted?"

"I know it is. It feels damned." Susan grinned. "The pipes make these weird noises. And sometimes there's this smell in the hallway and closets."

"The kind of a smell you can't pinpoint where it's coming from?"

"Exactly. Have you smelled that?"

"No."

Susan shuffled and cut the cards. "Because you're such a smart guy I'm only doing a one-card reading. Here, pick."

I pulled out the jack of hearts. I felt myself grow pale and looked at Susan.

"Well, that makes sense. It was once an all-male house." Maybe she was playing a trick on me. I knew she didn't like the fact that I was Rosie's boyfriend. Neither of Rosie's roommates did.

"Let me ask another question."

"It only works once."

"Stop being so sensitive." After knowing her for three years, I was tired of her constant attitude. "As if you're a real medium. Do three cards this time."

Susan rolled her eyes and shuffled the cards quickly. "Go ahead."

"Who is haunting our entryway?" Susan looked at me funny, but I insisted.

"Why don't you get yourself a Ouija board and leave me alone."

"Do you have one of those?"

"No."

"Then fucking deal the cards."

I could tell I was upsetting her. She was glaring at me, her eyes full of indignation and spite. I don't know how I could lose control like that, but it happened. I couldn't help myself. I was so full of suspicion. I could tell that Susan, like me, was tired. Tired of being pushed around by a bunch of assholes. That's where the sympathy stopped and started between the two of us.

After several angry seconds, Susan laid down three cards—the queen of spades, the jack of hearts, and the king of hearts. Something in my mind shifted when I saw this and I felt a spell of déjà vu coming on. She looked over at me, her eyes growing wider.

"Must be some sort of love triangle."

"Yeah, or the jack is tortured by his parents."

"Maybe the jack had a choice between a successful woman or a suicide king."

Susan cut the deck and then shuffled it together again. "You're reading too much into it. This guy was probably gay and hated his mother and father."

"I doubt it."

I looked at the cards and then up at the stairs. "Or he could have killed them both."

"That's cheery." Susan paused and I could see some sort of speech brewing inside her. "Rosie's been telling me about this dark cloud following you around."

"What business is it of yours?"

Susan frowned. "I just don't want any of your shit when it rains."

"Give me the cards."

"What's with your new interest in tarot?" Her words dripped with sarcasm, but I wasn't stopping now. Besides, I was very tired of her act and the shiv she kept putting between Rosie and me.

"Let me show you something about these cards." I got up from the floor.

"Get lost."

I surged toward Susan and snatched the deck of cards from her. "Watch this. My question is, who is rigging the cards?"

Susan looked completely terrified. She slowly backed her way towards her room. I shuffled, cut, and without looking down at the cards, pulled out the jack of hearts.

"Nice trick."

I shoved the cards towards her. "You do it."

"No, you're crazy. I hope Rosie doesn't put up with this."

I shuffled the deck again. "Watch closely. No tricks." I dealt three cards in a row—the jack of spades, the jack of hearts, and the jack of diamonds. "There's your gay love triangle."

"You're so creepy."

I threw the deck at her. "Go to hell."

Susan stomped away, flicked me off, and slammed the door to her room. I was so full of anger and I just wanted to lash out. When I could no longer hear her, I picked up the cards. The whole entryway gave me a nervous, morbid feeling. I finished collecting the cards, shuffled them, and pulled out one random card.

The jack of hearts.

It was him, I knew it. I walked up to the fourth floor and then climbed to the roof. The night was young, but already fog was rolling off the Charles like a cold, damp gauze. I drank the last of my beer and started to lay out the cards in threes on the roof ledge. I could feel the anger flowing within me like a current. I was determined to set things right. I had to know what had happened the previous night. I had to rid myself of suspicion.

For hours I dealt, shuffled, and dealt again. Occasionally I heard noises from the far corners of the roof, but saw nothing. I sat on the roof ledge for a long time. My anger grew into a burn. Around four in the morning, with all of Cambridge safely asleep, I dealt three jacks again.

I looked up. He was standing by the side of the chimney.

Good morning," he said.

"Not really," I said.

"What's wrong with you?" He smiled knowingly. "Girl troubles?"

"Who are you?" I was furious, but I wasn't going to let him know that yet.

"I'm the only one you can trust."

"Who are you? Did we have a class together that we know each other from?"

"It was the exceptionally talented and gifted one. After all, this is the finest academic institution." He drew closer. He had a cigarette dangling from a hand that curled around a highball. Through the fog I couldn't quite make out what he was wearing.

I sensed what an unlucky chapter of my life this had

all begun—that I was at the edge of a cliff pondering how deep the sea would take my fall. I reeked of failure and self-doubt. I treated all of this like it was some sort of class or test—something my entire life I was accustomed to acing. I had to know myself better than him. I had to beat him. I couldn't fail again. Not after Billy. Not after what had happened to Maeve.

But what could I possibly achieve?

I tried to soak him up with my eyes, make some sense of his presence. His cheek and jaw bones seemed sunken and marble. He was hearsed in death, a shadow's shadow.

As I stared at him, I lost focus on the roof and the rest of my surroundings. The muted riffs of a clarinet and trumpet drifted over Adams and up through the night air lulling me into his thoughts.

"You're full of shit." He let the ice jingle against his glass. "But I should expect that from a college kid. You know what your problem is?"

"You?"

"Lack of charity. You don't, as they say, suffer fools gladly." He put his hand out somewhere before my shoulder. I became very uneasy. "You should learn to be kind, learn to trust more often."

"How am I supposed to trust you if you pretend to know everything about me? How kind are you? You won't even answer my questions."

He took a quick gulp from his drink, adding time to his reply. "The only reason for your paranoia is your paranoia."

His glare intensified and I tried to break out. Something wasn't right. I could feel some sickness, some cancer deep inside me. "You talk a lot to say little. Who are you?"

"Why should I tell you?" he shot back. "I like my anonymity and in turn knowing everything about you. It makes me as clear and clean as a mirror. I just observe and reflect you. Nothing else concerns me."

He took a couple steps away from me and towards the ledge. I flapped my arms against my sides. My hands were numb. They suddenly looked old and wrinkled. The cancer was growing—its venom seeping through my arms and chest, pooling at the back of my throat. This was real. He was real, and I was frustrated with his games. He was the murderer. I knew it. I just wanted to lash out.

But I didn't. I breathed deeply and concentrated on staying calm. "Do you go to school here? Do you live in Adams House?"

"I did. Yes." He looked down at his shoes that blended into the mire of roof tar. For only the second time he became distant in response to something I had said. He lifted the highball into the dark night, studying the notches and facets of the crystal. "You could say I've drowned my sorrows here."

He was standing closer to the backlight of the streets. I could now see that he was wearing a dark gray suit. His tie was narrow and solid black. His jacket tapered to the waist and matched the stiff shortness of his French cuffs and handkerchief.

Then I knew he was someone from the past, and also someone very familiar. His clothing and his manner were odd, like something from an old detective movie. I felt resigned to his answers and half expected them. It was as if we were both reading from a script. I picked up the deck of cards and started throwing them, one by one, into the night sky.

"So what do the three jacks mean?" I moved slightly closer to him. Close enough to touch.

"Exactly what you think." He stepped back and raised his arms, allowing me to take him all in. He was continually smiling, which disturbed me. "I'm always having two men fighting over me. Call it what you will, I'm just pooling my resources."

I couldn't tell how much he was leading me on and so I played dumb. "I wouldn't have guessed that about you. Then again, I don't have the radar."

"But you seem to have the inclination, my dear boy. Even though I see you up here with women all the time."

He was baiting me. It struck me all right there—the emotions, the deceit, the two of us standing alone. Me talking to him. It was impossible, but here it was happening. And he was the one trying to control me, attempting to trap me with fear and suspicion. I tried to return the favor and stepped up within inches of him.

I looked him in the eye. "You're not very clever for someone who roams the night. Seeing how you're privy to everything I do in this dorm, you're shockingly stupid."

"Watch your mouth," he hissed.

"Sorry. Go back to drinking, you lush." I was getting to him. I could sense the anger and hate rising in him, almost as if I were feeling it in my own veins. I had primed him to blurt out something. Something that would upend my doubt and guilt.

He threw his glass over the roof and we heard it crash onto Bow Street. His neck seemed to bulge and shake from under his collar. The anger flashed like lightning across his face, and then he composed himself almost instantly. He eyed me intently. "You think you understand everything but you really know only two things: what I let you know and that you fear me."

"Who the hell are you?"

"I'm Maeve's new boyfriend."

"Go fuck yourself. I'm tired of your smoke and mirrors."

"Why don't you just turn yourself in? You raped her and killed her in the tunnel."

"No I didn't. It was you."

"Who, me? A figment of your imagination? Oh please. Drag me to the police. I'll confess." He turned his back to me. "I am your own tears and crashing hopes. I might have drowned my sorrows once, but that doesn't concern you. You should be careful of what pools inside you. You're distracted and broken from the truth, old friend."

"You give me nothing but round answers. I'm going to find out what happened and you're going to be the first person to help me."

"Like you helped Billy? I don't think so." His words stabbed at me for what they claimed to know. "Why should I help you? You are a fucking pervert. The way you raped and cut her."

I was completely shocked by what he knew, what he was hinting at. But no, it couldn't be. It was all guesses. He was just prodding my own fears, looking for a weakness. And the longer we spoke, the more I loathed him, and the more furious I was with myself.

I was so very tired of his sick games that it became too much. I charged at him. "Go to hell!"

I seized his arm. My grasp of him felt real but his skin was cold and soft, almost waxen. He spun around, looked at me quizzically, and began to laugh.

I can't describe the futile madness I felt holding him.

My hand on his arm had completed some sort of doomed and deranged circuit. I stood there frozen in that grasp.

Suddenly, his face fell out of laughter and began to melt and tear apart. I tried to pull back, but was frozen in fright, my arm clenched to his. His face then began to resolve, the features cohering into a familiar mold. I saw Maeve standing before me covered in blood, skinless and boiled to death. I could feel the heat stinging her body, my arm burning with her through those seconds of agony she faced in the tunnel. Her lips were burned and torn away, revealing glistening, hideous teeth with blood pooling and dripping from the gaps and gums. Whether they were clenched in anger or a smile I could not tell.

Horrified and sickened, I closed my eyes. As I pulled my arm away I felt a greater force—a near-silent, humming shock of electricity ran through my body. I remember nothing more and must have passed out entirely.

Chapter 16

I woke the next morning huddled in a corner of the roof. The difference those days between sleep and waking was vague and little. The cold that had been nagging me of late had become full-blown. A fever kept my mind gliding along a distracted, nervous path and prevented any deep sleep or break from the reigning confusion of the past few weeks. It was thirty degrees outside, but I was sweating profusely. A hacking cough couldn't cut the wheeze out of my chest.

I climbed down from the roof and shuffled off to my room. I thought about taking a hot bath but fell down on my sheetless, barren mattress instead. I tried to sleep but I kept going over my conversation with him. I had a better sense of what he looked like. But again I felt that my memory was failing me, as if I had met him many years before, and was now trying to pick out the details. I realized bitterly that I was just playing into his game. I had to find him somehow.

A small part of me hoped that if I ignored him at this point, I could cut my losses. Maybe I could have dropped some classes and sicked out of exams. But as I placed hope in these ideas, I remembered the trail of blood from Maeve to me. And I was sure that trail had been set down by him. If I could only discover his motive. I suspected even then that there wasn't one. I tried to push him out of mind, but that only left room for Maeve and a sinking feeling that the police were making their way to me. I needed to straighten him out before I lost control.

I rose from the bed, put on a new shirt, and headed down to the dining room. I picked up a copy of the daily paper. No news of Maeve, and it had been two days. It went to show that anyone could be dead or missing at that damn school and no one would notice. Her roommates probably thought she was holed up in the library. Then again, maybe the police were trying to track down her killer by keeping it out of the papers. Her killer? Listen to me. It was a freak accident, nothing more. But who else can say that besides me? I tried and failed once more to remember exactly who had seen us that Halloween night.

I walked out of Adams and over to the Yard. The crowds of people buzzing their way across the quads made me realize that it was Monday and I was missing another week of classes. I trudged through the Yard and on to Cambridge Street, where I bought a cup of coffee. It was a dull, wintry day and I soon wished I had a pair of gloves. I looked down at my hands, which were red and callused from the cold air. I barely recognized them in this condition. I felt things were changing about me and I wasn't even looking. My hands looked so old. I could see hundreds of tiny crevices that had once been smooth. I balled my hands into fists and blew on them to keep warm.

I came upon some sort of five-and-dime/drugstore stuck between an electronics bodega and a supermarket. I looked up at the sign—Skinnerian Apothecary. The sign was in an old-style script that reminded me of a Campbell's soup can. The front window was filled with wigs and walkers. The settled dust on everything reminded me of taxidermy at the natural history museum. And this was the youngest building on the block. I stood there for a few minutes staring into the front window as teenagers swarmed out of the Rindge & Latin school nearby. It was only a matter of time. I was at the end of youth. This decaying storefront was a window of what was to come. I turned back on Cambridge Street and went through a small park next to the public library. To my left was a row of thick pines that wound their way around the library. I heard a scratching noise and then nothing. My suspicions mounted. Across and down Broadway, I noticed a man sitting in a nondescript car paying close attention to his side mirror. I felt sure I was being followed—someone was dodging corners and hiding off the path. I didn't know if it was him or the police. I picked up my pace and started back towards school. Two Cambridge police cars came swimming along Ware Street and fished down Broadway. It was a very cold day and the hour for classes had started. Nonetheless, there were an unusual number of people hanging out around the back steps of Sever Hall. Each one of them gave me a suspicious sideways glance. I scurried past the back of Sever and into center of the Yard. I was dizzy and feverish, but certain that I was being lured into a trap. I darted across the main quad and up the steps to Widener Library. Once inside, I climbed the main staircase to the circulation floor and ducked into the stacks. I took the stacks elevator down to B-level. I crossed over to the west side of the building and hopped down the stairs to D-level. Past several stacks of dusty and corroding books, I hid behind a carrel with a view of the east-side passageway. If someone was following me, I could safely see him coming.

Ten, fifteen minutes later, no one had passed by or even come down to D-level. It was so quiet there I could hear pages being turned and chairs dragged forward into carrels several floors above. The decrepit stack elevator moaned and whined its way up the east side of the building, the brakes snapping at various floors. Sirens carried from Mass Ave and I tensed up for a moment as I imagined the police surrounding the library. I sat at the carrel desk, exhausted from just walking. I had to be careful, but now it seemed I was only betraying myself in fear. I had to calm down and think straight.

The steam pipes started to clank and hiss. Their gruesome, bending wails drew me into a panic. I couldn't take it. Feeding my anxiety, I realized that a mere thirty yards through the wall behind me lay the tunnels and crawl space where Maeve had died.

I waited another ten minutes. making sure no one had followed me. D-level was dim and silent. I thought of Maeve, and her radiant, blissful face. I pictured a dark, boiling wave of water and steam rushing in and drowning out her screams.

Drowning. The previous night came back to mind, and I remembered him talking about drowning his sorrows.

Was he talking about Maeve? Drowning, drowning his sorrows here?

And pooling. Pooling his resources. What pools inside me. I looked up at the steam pipes and traced them in my mind back to Adams House. He had drowned a long time before, I could feel it—I knew it better than any details of his face or what he had said the previous night. He had repeated the words, he was hinting at it, trying to be clever. Then I remembered that these pipes and the tunnels ran by the ground floor of B-entry and fed into the Adams House pool. Had he drowned someone else there? The tunnels ran right under the pool. A nervousness began to leap and fall in the pit of my stomach. The pool was where he had drowned.

I came out from behind the carrel and took the stacks elevator back up to the circulation level. I crossed the reading room over to the archive stacks for periodicals. I wandered through these dark, dusty cages, unsure where to start until I came to back issues of the College daily. The papers were bound by year in oversize red jackets. The College daily was started in the 1870s and there were four entire stack sections devoted to back issues. I ran my fingers over the spines of books. Where was he from? And when? Although I kept losing my memory of him, I felt close now to some vague truth of why this was happening. As I touched those oversized red folios, I could sense the time and history collapsing between us. It was an extraordinary feeling that I can barely describe and do not understand.

It was a lethal, wicked feeling.

Next to the stacks and along the back wall of the room was a computer terminal with a search for the College daily. I logged in and keyworded for "Adams" and "drowning." Nothing came up. I then searched for "pool" and "Adams" and found an article that dated the construction of the Westmorely pool as finished in 1935. The construction was a small part of a bigger College revitalization that gave jobs during the Depression. The database was complete through the 1990s, and other than that initial mention, there was nothing else about the pool or about anyone ever drowning in it.

I wandered back to the dusty archive shelves and pulled down the 1935 volume. I scanned for stories on the pool, and found two. The first concerned its opening and the second was about "honorary doctor of aeronautics" Charles Lindbergh taking a dip during commencement week. This second story was not mentioned in the database and tipped me off to the fact that there was more than what was listed by the computers.

I then looked in the 1936 and 1937 books. I kept searching up into the 1940s, finding only the occasional mention of the pool or Adams House. I pored over each day, unsure what I was looking for but compelled to continue. Something about searching through those years was eerily familiar to me. The more I searched, the more of what I found there felt remembered. As I got to the war years, the paper dropped off its frequency to once or twice a week. I scanned these years quickly, hoping to catch up in time to some unknown event. I kept on, feeling closer and closer to what I wanted to find. And I was desperate to find it. Through a filthy porthole window across the stacks, I noticed that it was already late evening and my search had exhausted several hours.

It was then that I opened the 1946–47 volume of the College daily. Most of the reports in the fall were about the "abhorrent deluge" of war veterans in their early twenties who were finally going to college on the GI Bill. Apparently, the ivory tower was being rattled by these older, middle-class students and the College was far from gracious about accepting veterans. Incidents of suicide and alcoholism rose dramatically. There were a few pleas for sympathy and respect, but overall the administration wanted nothing to do with this glut of former soldiers, airmen, and marines. One story listed Adams House as one of the remaining cloisters of blue-blood housing.

I was extremely tired and my anxiety to find something was subsiding. I was almost ready to give up. My eyes were glazing over October 1946 when I spotted a small article that appeared to be lifted from the police blotter and mildly rewritten.

> Three seniors drowned in the Adams House pool on the night of the 31st. The men were discovered at four in the morning by campus police locking down after the house's traditional Halloween party. Two of the men, Rockland Weir and Aaron Crossmud, were found with their wrists slit in what investigators believe to be a double suicide. The other, Daniel Edmonds, apparently drowned in an attempt to pull Weir and Crossmud from the pool. All three were residents of the house.

I swiped a pencil from a nearby carrel and wrote down the names of the three men on a scrap of paper. I scanned forward into November and December, and then January and February 1947, for more accounts of the drowning, but as I suspected, none were to be found. The administration and the families must have hushed the story. A cold sweat started coming on. It was on Halloween. The coincidence was unsettling, and the scarcity of specifics was depressing and familiar. There had to be a connection to what had happened to Maeve.

I closed the book and left the periodicals room. I recrossed the reading room and went back into the main stacks. Having shelved in the library for over three years, I knew the old yearbooks were on the west side of the sixth floor. I sped up the stairs. I snatched the 1947 yearbook from the shelf and looked for their names. None of them appeared in that year's book. I looked through the group house and team pictures but they weren't in any of those either.

I tried the 1946 yearbook, but there were few mentions of the junior class and no photos. I left the sixth floor and took the elevator to B-level. I crossed from the west side of the library to the east. Through the stacks on that side of B-level was a tunnel to Lamont Library. The tunnel was about fifty yards in length, with several steam pipes hanging from the ceiling and its side. The tunnel was painted a jaundiced yellow that had cracked and peeled. It was more direct and much quicker than surfacing, walking the path through the Yard, and then showing ID again to the Lamont attendant. As I turned the corner into the east side of B-level, I saw a campus security guard and a librarian standing in the entrance to the tunnel.

At their feet were dozens of ripped books. They looked up at me, and I froze.

"Where are you going?" the security guard asked.

After several seconds I managed to say, "Lamont."

"Have you seen anyone down here that might have done this?"

For years the College's libraries had been haunted by a book slasher. I had just heard of him, and though the dark stacks of Widener were a den of etiolated weirdos, I had never seen him or any slashed books. The last slashing had been years before I was around, but here before the three of us was proof that he was still making his rounds.

My throat went completely dry as I coughed up the first lie that came into my head. "I just came from the circulation floor. I haven't been in the stacks at all today."

The two looked at each other. I couldn't tell if they were wasting time or trying to take in every detail. After a few moments, though, the guard checked my ID and waved me by.

I hurried past them and ran to the Lamont end of the tunnel. I was close to a complete breakdown. Sweat was pouring from my temples and the back of my neck. I started coughing uncontrollably. It was him, I knew it. They weren't after me, and he was just toying with me—trying to fluster me into giving myself away for what he'd done. He had followed me all day and was now setting me up at every turn.

At the basement entrance to Lamont, I stopped to calm down and regain my poise. I stood there for several minutes while I grew more and more fearful of my next step. My breathing had dropped again into an aggravated wheeze. I wasn't going to let him wear me down, though. I started climbing the long stairwell out of the basement. As I turned around at the first mid-landing, I looked back at the library tunnel entrance.

And there was Michael coming through the doors from the tunnel. His backpack was off his shoulder and he was clutching it to his chest with both hands. He looked back down the tunnel for a second and then turned to see me on the mid-landing. He looked completely unsurprised, as if expecting to find me there. I was still breathing hard and leaned back against the wall watching him.

"Hey man, where have you been?" he asked and took a couple steps up the stairs toward me. "I lost track of you at the dance."

"Just studying," I managed to say between breaths. This was more than coincidence. Michael was the only other person who had an inkling about Maeve and me. He may have had his own reasons to see us together or have Rosie catch me. No, he was a friend and I was scared.

"Why are you here?" I finally asked.

"I'm looking for Happy, we're studying together, but I forgot where to meet her." He kept methodically climbing the stairs, his bookbag still in both arms. "Did you see the slashed books?" he asked with almost too much puzzlement in his voice.

"Did you do that?" I spit back at him. I couldn't breathe right. The stairwell was filled with stagnant air. I had to get out.

Michael laughed. "Yeah, I'm your man, officer." There was something very rehearsed about all of this.

"Why are you here?" I repeated, more suspiciously this time. I took a couple steps up and away from him. The sweat was dripping from me now. I felt grimy and suffocated.

"Are you all right?" Michael was now at the mid-landing and a few yards away from me. "Are you sick?"

"Stop following me!" I yelled back.

"Take it easy." Michael put his backpack down on the

mid-landing. I thought of the blood I had cleaned from my room. All the blood.

"Go away." Every sound in the stairwell echoed and echoed. I grabbed my face, ready to gouge it out. "Stop it." I backed away from Michael.

"Let me help you." He reached out to touch my arm.

I had to get away. I had to breathe. "If you want Rosie, you can have her." I ran up the stairs away from him. "Just leave me alone."

I looked back one last time and saw Michael methodically turn and reach into his backpack. My last comment had pissed him off, but he seemed set on something else. I raced up to the main floor of Lamont.

I bolted through a set of doors and stood there trying to figure out what was wrong with me. I tried to catch my breath and control my fear. Being scared was only giving myself away. I had to stop all of this from getting out.

I went directly to the reference section in search of the freshman facebooks. I found the 1942-43 edition and looked up Rockland Weir, who hailed from Greenwich, Connecticut. His face was not familiar, and neither was Aaron Crossmud's. Then I came to Daniel Edmonds. It was a fuzzy, time-worn photo, but it looked like him—dark combed-back hair, and that same chin line.

A panic washed over me as I realized he came from the same prep school as me. I started to shake uncontrollably, dropping the facebook. He was stalking me. But he was not alive. He was a memory forgotten and ignored by everyone except me.

That day, I had dug up way too much to know what it all meant. The pieces of the puzzle were not fitting. All I knew was this: bound in violence to that place, he now tormented me.

My fever shot back up in this wave of panic and I felt faint. I picked up the facebook again and ripped out Daniel Edmonds's page. I rushed out of the library and headed straight for Adams House.

When I returned to Adams that day, autumn was veering into winter. Disaster seemed imminent. Things at school were falling apart, yet life felt strangely abstract—as if I were watching a movie of myself taking each precarious, inevitable, and stupid misstep. And I was tired, almost past the point of caring.

But another irrespective part of me was cutting to the chase. I was addicted to the self-pity. At the same time, I thought the trip to the library had sharpened my understanding. I had a sense of who he was. Even if I was foolishly convinced of my upper hand in dealing with him.

For the next two weeks, I kept a vigil on the roof of Adams House. At first, I didn't intend to sit up there waiting for him, but the stairwell and my room felt marked and creepy and those places somehow blocked my concentration. Perched on the roof I had advance warning if the cops did show up or if anyone else came up B-entry. I wanted to be away from everyone; from all the selfishness and pettiness that I had grown accustomed to for over three years. Deep down, I wanted to suffer for what had happened to Maeve.

I also felt that I could draw my problems out onto that roof and erode any anxieties or delusions by facing him. So I began to stalk him and cloister myself—inhabiting the night, waiting for the shadows to come together and make sense.

My cold worsened into bronchitis in the freezing and dank New England air. As the nights wore on, the waiting put a delirious, ascetic spell over my habits. I went to the dining room at the crack of dawn each day to load up on food. I avoided all contact with others in the house. Like some sick beast, I grunted at or shied from those who recognized me as they passed by in the halls. Rosie left messages under my door on several occasions, all of which I ignored. On her last visit she left a note to the effect that I was a conniving, selfish fuck and dropping off the face of the earth as I had done was the best thing that had ever happened to her. The note had a cleansing effect. By ridding myself of connections, I felt pure. I had no love left. Maeve didn't deserve to die. I had to change. I forgot about my classes and was absent for my midterm makeups. A week into my vigil, a letter from the dean was pushed under my door. I was on academic probation. I didn't shave or shower. I became the mess I'm now known as.

On the roof I constructed a makeshift shelter by the old water tower. I sat in the cold every night until four or five in the morning, waiting and watching. I wore three sweaters and a down coat, but my exposed face and hands were soon windburned and bright red. I bought two cartons of cigarettes with the last of my savings. Anything else I needed I charged to my parents, which was their only evidence that I was still alive. I barely ate, and when I did, it was all cereal and coffee. In the late hours, I alternated shots of cold medicine and Cuervo to dull the pain in my chest and head.

On November 10, almost two weeks since the night I last saw her, Maeve's picture appeared in the paper. The article was mainly quotes from her roommates, who mistakenly thought she had gone home. This was followed by almost blithe reactions from her parents, who had assumed she was studying hard or sneaking around New York visiting friends. Reading the story brought a new sense of permanence to her death. Such a gorgeous, intelligent girl—it was depressing how little anyone really seemed to care, how little it mattered. The article claimed the police had several leads.

Did I even care? I thought I did. Until I saw that story, I had almost convinced myself that her death was a bad dream. Now the full burden was on me. I had to stay away. Otherwise they would see the guilt on my face, in my eyes.

I scanned the remainder of the paper. Midterms and MCATs had resulted in three more suicides among the senior class. The university hospital was out the door with manics turning depressive. The administration was proud to announce its "challenging" fund-raising goals for the coming year.

Nearly two weeks had passed and there was still no sign of him. It was another Friday night and the College had given everyone a three-day weekend in honor of Veterans Day. I was disgusted with myself and the futility of waiting up on that damn roof. I wandered through the entryway, ending up in front of my own room. Certainly I doubted myself. I doubted whether he was real, or whether I had just lost it. But as those doubts crept in, all I had to do was take two steps down the hall to the bulletin boards on each floor of B-entry. Over the past few days every kiosk and poster area on campus had been plastered with photos of Maeve. Missing. Information Wanted. During those cruel weeks, I couldn't stand looking at them. Posters, flyers, smudgy gray xeroxes of her freshman facebook photo everywhere. It was as if everyone was being let in on my guilt.

While my vigil may have seemed foolish, it was not because he wasn't real. The search for Maeve became my purpose and proof. I came to the conclusion each and every time: I was doing the right thing. I was out of touch with what was going on, but it seemed they were really searching for her and I couldn't believe the police hadn't come by to talk to me. But then I realized that Maeve didn't live in Adams and she had been in costume that night. It was possible people had seen me with her, but assumed that she was Rosie.

I opened the French doors of my room and stepped out onto the small balcony. From there I watched the last few students trickle away for the holiday. I felt sleepy and drifted back into my room to lie down. The silence of the emptied hallways comforted me—I was truly alone without forcing withdrawal or ducking away.

I dragged on a cigarette and morosely pondered the events of the semester. As I traced over the first time I saw him and then that last night with Maeve, my thoughts ranged from blurred to defiant. I just needed some rest. For a moment I couldn't remember anything—my parents, my childhood, Rosie. I had become bitter and I knew it.

I was exhausted from my vigil and my eyelids sank heavily. The mattress in my room was still sheetless, but I didn't care anymore. I stabbed out my cigarette and lay back, anxious yet weary. I thought about that horrible Halloween night and about what had happened to Daniel Edmonds. There had to be a way to know, and the more I considered it, the more things pointed to the tunnels.

I had to find where he lurked and coax him out. That was the deluded plan, at least. I put on my coat, grabbed the hammer from my desk drawer, and left my room. I had to undo things—set the course straight before everyone came back from the long weekend. I would go back into the steam tunnels to lure him out somehow. I could feel his presence growing in me even while thinking about what I would do. I could see him, even when he wasn't physically there. And that night, the vision grew and became very strong. He was a creature of habit, and I understood that. I was becoming one too. I had to find out what had happened to Maeve, and if possible, discover something I could come forward with as evidence.

As casually as I could, I ambled down the stairs. What if they were watching me? What if the police were waiting for me to lead them to her? Halfway down, I lurched to a stop. I listened closely. B-entry was utterly still. I scampered down some more stairs and looked out the windows on the second-floor landing. The courtyard and rooms across from me were pitch black. The early night sky was hazy and bronze. If I could make it to the basement and then duck into the tunnel, maybe I could elude their watch. They were probably waiting outside the entry doors for me. If I stayed inside, I could do it. I had to know more. I had to find him.

I tiptoed past the pool. The dark cedar and frosted glass of the door seemed grave, portentous. I thought to duck inside there for a moment, but found the door locked. So I made for the basement and the short hallway to the tunnel door. I listened for someone following me. The silence, as so many other times in that awful place, did not feel like an absence, rather something hushed and full.

I slammed at the lock with the hammer. Four, then five quick blows around the cylinder and I was able to pry the lock out of the dented door. I headed into the steam tunnel. It was darker than I remembered, and I stood there for a few minutes shivering in fear, waiting for my eyes to adjust. The steam murmured at a low level, the school's use down for the holiday. It was still hot and sweat beaded on my temples almost instantly. I walked, again hunched slightly, in the direction of Mass Ave. The smell was rancid and familiar. Each step, each breath of that fetid air brought me closer to that night.

My eyes welled with tears as I hobbled along silently. In the sections of utter darkness I imagined Maeve's beautiful eyes and hair. I recalled our night at the Advocate together. I remembered standing in line unnoticed, watching her. Her lips so sweet and tremulous, I could almost taste them in the darkness.

I tried my pockets for a lighter or matches but didn't find any. The tunnel was incessantly winding and bending back, and I passed many side valves and offshoots. I kept going for what must have been fifteen minutes. I began to worry. I should have come upon the Mass Ave crawl space by now. I looked back into the thick blackness of the tunnel. I didn't see any doors or lit spaces to exit from. Where the hell was I?

I began to jog along, looking for some landmark. My feet splashed along in the constant trickle on the tunnel floor. A broad side tunnel came up on my right. I stopped, and as the noise around me thinned out, I heard a dying laugh.

It could have been a pipe bending with steam or a subway vent carrying distant track clatter. It could have been anything. But I heard the whispers and closeness of a laugh and knew it could also be him. I followed the noise down the side tunnel. I was so nervous I had almost anticipated this lead. It was him. I could tell by that unsure mix of anger and fear in my chest.

For my first few steps I crept along attempting to be noiseless. Then I heard the laugh again, this time more distinct yet farther away. I thought of the story I had found in the paper. The pool. The suicides. It was an angle, not the truth being told. The reporter may have even believed it, but it was a line—a list of ifs—taken as fact.

I began to jog through the subtunnel, going faster and faster. My back and the nape of my neck were burning from the constant scrapes against the tunnel's ceiling. My lungs were raw and tight as I tried to suck oxygen out of that stagnant, moist air. I must have run a good forty yards. And I kept running. And with each pace I thought I heard laughter fall in between.

I was certain I was closing in on the sound when I ran straight into a metal door. I fell back. The door wobbled loudly and thousands of rancid, teetering water drops fell from the ceiling onto me. I had luckily hit the door in stride, my foot curling into it, then my head and body.

Still, I was dazed and having extreme trouble breathing. I stood up and searched the darkness around the door. The lightbulb above it was out. I tapped at it and it flickered on. The stencil on the door told me it was an entrance to Houghton Library.

But that was impossible. I couldn't have crossed Mass Ave. I was certain that the crawl space was the only way over the subway and under the avenue. Something wasn't right.

The light burned out. I tried the doorknob, and while the big metal door was rusted and stuck, the knob turned. I stood back and kicked at the door. Each kick was filled with a dumb rage, often missing the spot at which I was aiming. After a dozen tries, I heard the rusted seal crack. I turned the knob again and the door opened enough for me to slide through.

I came up into the subbasement of Houghton, climbed a flight of stairs, and entered the archive. I had to be careful—Houghton was full of bugs and alarms. Most of them, though, were upstairs, where the rare folios and manuscripts were kept. If I stayed away from the elevators and display cases, I would be all right. It must have been close to midnight but all the lights in the archive were on. Coming out of the darkness of the tunnels, this place was too antiseptic and bright. I found a carrel and plunked down to catch my breath. I sat still for a moment and listened. I hadn't heard his laughter since I entered the library. He could go upstairs where I would never find him. But he was playing his games—he needed me to some extent—and I was convinced he wasn't that far. It occurred to me then to check the archive for more about Daniel Edmonds. I knew they kept records on each class. And there was also Z stacks.

Z stacks, which was part of the movable stacks, was only reshelved by the librarian. There were a lot of rumors floating around about what was in Z stacks. I once heard it held the largest prewar French pornography collection in North America, which some nutjob professor had accumulated over the years. But then I also remembered another shelver telling me that Z stacks was where they filed away anything damaging that related to the College.

I got up from the carrel and walked down the aisle that held the movable stacks. Z stacks was at the end of the row. The fluorescent lights intermittently purred and whined; my step was dampened by the thin carpet. I reached Z stacks and pressed the green button. The stacks didn't move. I had forgotten that I needed the supervisor's key. I still had my hammer and thought about busting the lock. But that would be useless—the system was electronic. I tried to recall where the stacks supervisor would leave the key.

Suddenly, all the lights in the archive went out.

I crouched, not knowing what else to do. The green light on the row for Z stacks began flashing red. I had to get out quick, maybe back through the tunnel. I stood up. I heard a slight noise, papers rustling. A match sparked and ignited a few feet in front of me. Out of the crackling light I saw his face.

He was grinning maniacally from ear to ear. I moved back against the wall, completely stunned and terrified that he had cornered me. He held the match delicately between two fingers. He brought the flame closer to his face, the shadows of his jaw and forehead becoming more obtuse and monstrous. In his other hand he had a fistful of papers.

"Are you after these?" he asked, smiling and coy. He brought the match to the papers. "You're so nosy. It's going to get you in trouble."

I took a step towards him. "Why are you doing this?"

"We all must suffer. But I want an accounting for our sins. Do you understand?" He hissed the last of these words. The papers started to catch.

"But why me?"

"Stop being such a fool." He pushed the red light of Z stacks. The row moved open slightly and he threw the burning papers in and then pushed the button again to close the row. I knocked at his arm, trying to stop him. Then I pitched forward, vainly trying to rescue the papers from the shelf. The heat blew across my hand and I snatched my arm back just before the row closed on it. I was too late. He watched idly, bemused.

"You'd better leave, before they come," he said.

"I'm not leaving until you tell me why." My burned hand bloomed and flared in pain.

"You know well enough," he replied in a stern yet almost serene voice. "Go."

I had a grave, intimate sense of him then—as if a memory, or some close understanding, was picked from a long-forgotten dream. The fire had caught. The old magazines, photos, and files of Z stacks began to snap, hiss, and burn.

"You're coming with me." I reached for his arm. He flew back down the aisle like a wave of dark water. I tried to follow him.

"In the morning, things will be different," he said.

All the lights for the archive floor came back on. I squinted and shielded my eyes. The sprinklers came on, gurgling and pounding with air, then water. When I looked up, he was gone. An alarm sounded that was deafening. I looked back quickly at Z stacks engulfed in black smoke, then I ran out of the archive and down the stairs to the basement. I entered the steam tunnel and sped down to the main tunnel section. But I couldn't remember which way to go. I finally chose left, running as fast as I could, certain they would find me. I could hear the bastard laughing at me. Echoes far and near bounced around me. Had they picked up my trail already? The alarm must have been silent at first. I looked back and saw pins of light coming into the main tunnel section. I shoved on as fast as I could, my back stinging in pain. I skidded along a slight downslope and tripped on a pipe. My head hit first. I was coming in and out and could taste my blood seeping down in the runoff. My eyes gave into the darkness. The minutes crawled like hours. The echo of their footsteps was growing. They would find me soon. Maybe I should give up. It would be better to end it.

But then I woke up, startled and on the roof of Adams House.

Chapter 18

If it was a dream, I was still terrified that they would find me. But it couldn't have happened. I was exhausted and delusional. My dreams were coming from deep within, dreams of shame and sadness. That's what made it seem so real. From the roof, I watched dawn curl up and over the night. Two weeks into my vigil, I was still bereft of any answers.

A few more days passed. I was almost too sick to keep going. During the daytime I would return to my room. There I slept on my barren, bleach-soaked mattress only waking to cough or throw up. My message machine had over a dozen blinks, so I unplugged the phone. I knew a couple of the messages were from Michael, but how could I confide in him now? He had his own agenda now—namely Rosie. During my nights on the roof, I would often sit on the north side above A-entry with a full view of the B-entry stairwell. Twice I saw him creep up to her room. To study? Well, then, why did they wait for Happy and Susan to leave before he came over? Whatever idiotic class they had in common sure took a lot of studying, particularly when finals were weeks away. Oh yes, the two of them must have studied very hard. It enraged me to think that my friendship with Michael had been one big scheme to get to Rosie. I should have gone down there and caught the two of them, but I didn't want to stir Michael's suspicion that I had anything to do with Maeve's disappearance. That Halloween night he was probably too drunk to remember what happened, but nonetheless, I had talked to him about Maeve and he could point the police my way. In fact, I'm surprised he hadn't confronted me about it. I suspected that Michael's staying quiet meant he didn't want to draw my attention to Rosie and him. As long I wasn't around, things were good.

But what did it matter then? I had to make the choice to help myself. I had to separate myself from others—I had to clear my head.

On November 17, the papers reported that the police had traced Maeve to the masquerave but no one there remembered who she was with. They were getting closer—at least twenty people that night must have seen me with Maeve. I couldn't believe they hadn't come to interview me yet.

That's when I was called in to see Master Donahue. The note was shoved under my door one morning.

Please schedule an appointment with the House secretary immediately. I need to discuss something with you. Best, Donahue

I must have read that note a hundred times trying to discern whether he knew something or not. The word "immediately" seemed ominous enough. But overall, I thought the note was too nice, as if I were up for an award. Dozens of possibilities and inferences raced through my head. They knew. It was a trap to catch me. But if I didn't go, then they would know I was guilty. Even if Donahue didn't know, he would begin to suspect something.

But if they really weren't on to me, what the hell else could it be? They'd already put me on academic probation. I spent the rest of the day pounding at my temples, trying to figure it out. Eventually exhaustion and common sense came through. If Donahue or the police knew about my connection to Maeve, they wouldn't tip me off this way. They would bang down my door, not request a social call.

I phoned Donahue's secretary and scheduled an appointment for the following morning. I spent the entire night up, partly worried I'd sleep through the meeting, and partly convinced that I should run away. I drank countless cups of coffee attempting to stay clear on matters. By the time of the meeting, I had sufficiently calmed down and perked up.

So I headed over to Apthorp and was led through to the rear of the house, where Donahue's office was. His secretary sat me down in a dark green leather chair across from his desk. She left and I heard her walk down the hall to get Donahue. I waited. There were some files on his desk. I was tempted to look and rose slightly from my chair. If it was Maeve I was there for, I could still make it out through the back door and into the garden.

And then I thought that he could be watching. I sat back down.

If I acted suspicious, then they would *be* suspicious. I searched the room for a camera but found only the normal collegiate accouterments. There was an Adams bust behind his desk. Lord knows which one—they all had that same mole-ish Pilgrim squint. Tired and inattentive, I gawked at the bronze bust for a while. It was the color of an old penny. I tried to remember if I'd ever seen a bust of someone still alive. I couldn't think of any and concluded that busts were the aesthetic equivalent of death masks and profile portraits. Museums, the pyramids, libraries—dead history strewn and littered everywhere. Especially at the College, where it seemed that every lousy red brick was donated as a memorial and engraved with an epitaph.

I closed my eyes and pictured the memorial Maeve would get. Weeping parents, short poignant speeches. Then Maeve's bust would be revealed. Oh Jesus, what a dreadful thought. Maeve's soft face arrested in dark alloy and then slowly oxidized until no one remembered why she was important enough to have been bronzed in the first place. Within a few years, her bust would be pushed to the corner of the house library to watch the card catalog collect dust. Better yet, put it up on the roof of B-entry as a gargoyle.

I opened my eyes. Donahue's desk was a slab of darkly stained pine. I sat there for a moment staring at the knots and ridges in the front panel. I traced one knot with my finger, around and around the rings of its eye. He had an old brass inkwell on his desk. In the center, an eagle stooped over the jars. Military surplus, I guessed. I could picture the general who'd owned it once. I bet he had two silly little flags poking from it. Donahue, however, kept a letter opener and an incense boat where the flags would be. On the side walls of the office ran portraits of former masters of the house. Each ashen figure was shrouded in a dark brown or gray suit. If I had gotten up from my chair, I'm sure their eyes would have followed. But for now the masters of Adams simply stared down, draconic, imperious.

Finally, I heard footsteps returning, and then Donahue entered the room. He smiled and took a seat next to me in another green chair. He looked me over for a few seconds, and for the first time I was truly embarrassed for having let myself go. Jeans and a dark shirt will go a long way, but I must have looked like a mess. He was sitting in front of his desk and very close to me. Was this a friendly chat? I was getting more nervous.

"I have just a couple of things to discuss with you," he began. I shook my head as if willing to comply. He thought for a second, then realized the files were on his desk. He reached over and grabbed the top file. He put on his glasses. They were the wrong ones. He got up from the green chair and went behind the desk, where he found his reading glasses in a drawer. I remembered from the seminar I had with him that he was prone to this bumbling. Regardless, Donahue was not stupid.

"So the dean has put you on probation. You know that, right?"

I nodded again. The muscles in my neck fell limp. It was just academics. A firm talking to and then a slap on the wrist. Thank God.

"Look. I know how bright you are. You wrote the best paper for my seminar last spring. It was on *Turn of the Screw*, and I forget what you were examining."

"Modes of storytelling."

"Right, right. Very good." His mouth was slightly agape, and I could tell it wasn't ringing a bell. "Now, this slip happens to a lot of seniors. They get tangled in the academic weeds." He opened the file. I swallowed.

"You haven't taken any midterms and have turned in only two of eight papers due." He said it with the open-ended lilt of a question.

"I know. I apologize." I was relieved to the point of flippant.

"Don't apologize." Donahue's voice was suddenly stern. "You haven't done anything to me. You're doing this to yourself. Getting in deeper and deeper. I just have to warn you that if this isn't made up before exams . . . well . . ."

"I understand. It's just that I've been so busy . . ." I looked again at the Adams bust. Halls of Fame. Baseball and football at least. They have busts of people still alive.

"Son, I know that this is a hard time for you. And I have to admit I'm a bit worried based on your appearance." He closed the file and took off his glasses. Was this the sympathy after the ultimatum? I liked Donahue, but enough with the act. "I talked to the dean's office and put in a word for you about this probation. If you make up all the work, they'll expunge the probation from your record."

"Expunge, sir?"

"Yes, retroactively remove it from your file. It's as if it never happened."

He put his hand on my knee, looking for gratitude and

concord. The more I learned about the College, the more it resembled the Ministry of Information. I trembled and rested my hands uncomfortably across my chest. The coffee was starting to lose the battle with exhaustion. I tried to look away from him. Stay calm, it's almost over. I put my head in my hands, embarrassed by this treatment.

"I know you're a smart kid, and I want to help. But you have to clean up and get cracking." He shook my knee, and I looked up. "Hey, it's all going to be over in a few months, right?" He smiled. Yeah, and then I wouldn't be your lousy problem anymore.

"Thanks," I managed to squeak and then sat up, readying to leave.

Donahue's hand pushed me back down into the chair. "Now there is something else we have to talk about." He said it casually, but I held my breath and watched him rise out of his chair. "Would you mind waiting here one second?"

He went to the door. I let out my breath and nervousness seized my chest. I turned toward the door.

"This is Detective Reilly and this is Detective Black. They're with the Cambridge police."

My neck wrenched up with pain. I forced a polite nod. I had been suckered. My heart was pounding. They knew. Of course they knew. My lungs felt sore and seemed to be grating at the sides of my ribs as I breathed. Donahue went behind his desk. My mouth dried almost instantly and I could feel the small sores on my tongue bristle against my teeth. Reilly sat in the green chair next to me. The other stood at the back of the room.

"The detectives just have a few questions for you." Donahue seemed very calm and fluid now. It had all been an act. They had me. "Now, you don't have to answer any of these questions if you don't want to. That's why I'm here. To make sure of that."

I broke into a fit of sneezing. I must have been allergic to something in that office. My eyes began to water. Donahue asked if I wanted something to drink. I shook my head no and sat up. I stared directly at Reilly. He wore the traditional flatfoot ensemble—brown raincoat, gray suit, and a blue tie that matched his eyes. I didn't get a very good look at Black, but he wore a dark raincoat. His eyes were hidden behind a fedora.

"Is it okay, son, if they ask a few questions?"

"Yes." Did I have any choice?

Reilly gave Donahue a brief, thankful look. He had pulled out his memo book and now looked it over. I wiped my hands into my pants. My palms were soaking wet.

Then Reilly asked: "You were William Thompkins's roommate freshman year, correct?"

Billy? I blurted a yes. I know Reilly saw the confusion in my face and made note of it. In fact, that's probably what saved me.

"And you were his roommate up until he committed suicide."

"Yes." My nose, my whole face, began to itch.

"And when did he do that?"

"Spring semester."

Reilly frowned slightly. "Could you be more specific?"

"April thirteenth." What were they getting at? Did Maeve know Billy somehow?

"Thank you." Reilly leafed through his memo book. "Would you say that the two of you were friends as roommates?"

"Yes, he was a good friend."

"Can you make any attempt at answering the question of why William committed suicide?"

"We called him Billy." My eyes were really watering now and I pulled a tissue from my pocket to dab at them.

"Then what was Billy's problem?" Reilly was very calm. Maybe I wasn't in trouble. Or maybe I was in so much trouble that they didn't have to force things.

"I don't know. I don't think anyone knows that."

"I know this is hard, but can you remember if he had any problems?"

"I don't know. He hid things from me, from all around him."

"Did he have fights with you or anyone?"

"Why are you asking me this?"

Reilly looked over at Black. Donahue thumbed at his files. I was on my own. Then Reilly put his memo book away. It was hard to tell if they were annoyed at me or the general lousiness of police work.

"There's been a fire. A fire in one of the libraries last weekend."

Black interrupted, "You work in the libraries, don't you?" He had a thick, impatient voice.

"Where was this fire?" Donahue asked.

"Houghton Library," Reilly answered.

"I work in Widener and Lamont libraries," I said and turned my shoulder to look over at Black. He had his back to me and seemed to be examining the portraits.

Reilly raised his hand to get my attention. "There was a fire in the archive. In the basement of Houghton."

I turned slowly back toward Reilly.

"We're sure that this incident was arson and we're trying to find our culprit."

So it was true. It had happened. Culprit. I couldn't believe this. Guilty by association. I was angry, but the fear was overwhelming. These men were policemen. Throw away the key. How? The tunnels. I had gone through the tunnels that night.

"The fire didn't really catch, though. There were only a few things damaged. But"—Reilly looked over at Black for agreement—"the arsonist used Billy's file as kindling."

"Oh my God," I stammered without thinking. Tears were streaming down my face. I wiped them away and tried to regain myself. Black was watching me do this. He knew. I wasn't facing him, but I could feel his eyes boring down on my back. "Sorry, I've got allergies." And I sniffed accordingly.

"You see, the person who burned Billy Thompkins's file destroyed the record of his classes, his grades, the College's account of what happened, and other personal information. The file was badly burnt except for one piece of paper which was overlooked or set aside for some reason. That piece of paper was a list of people interviewed after his suicide. So we're going down that list and asking if any of you"—Reilly folded his arms and sat back—"know who might have done this. Someone with a grudge against Billy. Someone who lived in your freshman dorm."

"No."

"Maybe Billy had some ex-girlfriends." The question was kind of throwaway. I didn't know if Reilly was suspicious or bored.

God who formed all things both rewardeth the fool, and rewardeth the transgressor.

"I said no. I said I don't know." They wanted to get me on the denial. They wanted to push me as far into this hole as possible.

"But are you sure?" Black bellowed.

"I'm sorry, but no." My tight breathing was leaving me light-headed. Edmonds was responsible. I could feel it. But how would he know about that? He couldn't have been watching me since freshman year. The tunnels. I went through the tunnels in my dream. Had he seen Billy too? But why would he care?

Black paced to the front of the room to look me in the eye. "Where were you over the weekend?" The question was surprisingly timid. He must know.

"I was here." Oh Lord help me. I couldn't look Black in the face. I felt like crying. It was all coming down. Trapped. "I was working . . ."

"Did you see anyone suspicious? Someone with a connection to Billy?" Black put his hand forward on the back of my chair and stood over me. I still couldn't look at him. I felt so ashamed, frightened.

"No," I murmured.

"Are you sure?" If I told Black now it would be all over. I should tell Black.

"Gentlemen, I think that's enough." Donahue stood up and walked around the desk. "He's said no several times."

Black rose up and took a step back from me. I looked at Reilly, who gave his partner a satisfied nod. He was giving up. Maybe I confused his contempt for me with his contempt for investigating a petty arson case. Reilly pleasantly thanked me for my time. Donahue showed them out. Sweat was streaming down my neck.

It was Billy's file he was burning, not his own. I was in a daze. I remember being there, but there's no way I could have gotten in. Besides, I don't recall any light, I would have brought a light down there. But there's no other way, no explanation. It was a dream. It had to be.

Donahue waited for them to leave. He thanked me somewhat apologetically and then led me out to the front door. I had to stop along the way to control my coughing.

"Are you sick, son? You look like hell."

"Yes and no." I had to leave that house before he started to suspect more.

"Get some rest and then catch up on your studies. And don't worry." We were both a step outside now. "I talked to them before you came in, and they think the connection to the Billy thing is some fluke. They just wanted to confirm that with you. They said not to worry. They'll catch the guy. It's just some disturbed person running around the libraries. Probably a former library employee with a grudge against the College. He'll slip up and slash some books on camera. They'll catch him."

I walked out of the sophomore quad and slithered across Plympton Street to the main entrance to Adams. A fluke or a test? They needed me to slip up, and more important, lead them to Maeve. I couldn't believe that I'd almost blown it like that. Then again, what good was arresting me if they had no proof, no recovered remains? I had to play it cool. I had to calm down. Hard to say if Donahue was in on it. I slipped through the tunnels to B-entry. But even so, why were they waiting? I climbed the stairs slowly, struggling for breath along the way. I was shaking from the ordeal and just wanted to hide. I reached the fourth floor and looked over at B-46. My stomach turned. I couldn't bear going in, the whole place made me claustrophobic. I climbed up to the roof for some air.

Chapter 19

It was becoming clear that I was being set up. Daniel Edmonds had started the fire knowing it would lead them to me. I had to catch up to him and quit hobbling around like a foolish monk. He had killed Maeve and blamed me. I had to step away from this ritual and reenactment. He was trying to live out 1946 and I had to break out of the trap of playing along.

But my early-morning watches had proved useless. It had been more than a week since I last saw him, and I was still unsure what I had even seen. From time to time, I felt someone or heard a movement across the roof's tar paper. He was trying to break my stamina and drive me crazy. I was persistent, though. As my hopes to catch him began to run thin, I would get caught in my anger and resentment of him. Something about him gave me the desire, the will, to watch.

On the morning of November 21, I was coming down off the roof for my early breakfast run. Just before, I had swallowed several Benadryl to keep my fever down and quaffed a bottle of Robitussin for my cough. Before I even reached the B-entry stairs I grew desperately weary and had to lie down. I reached down to the balustrade, which curved away from my grasp. I could tell by the static signal building in my head that I had overdosed on the medication. I stumbled back to my room. My circulation slowed until all I could hear was my own aggravated breathing. I looked around my dismal room. Cheap yellow shades were drawn over the French doors protecting the dark from the early morning. I had cleaned every inch of the room a dozen times but I could still smell a faint odor of blood and decay.

I closed my eyes and fell into a light, uncomfortable sleep. Out of the darkness came many erratic shapes and forms onto the back of my eyelids. I again listened carefully to my own wheezing breath as it staggered over each inhalation. The stars strobed and flared through the darkness. Bolts of red and blue light crossed over the shallow void. I slowly felt my eyes relax and give in to the blindness of sleep. And just as I was drifting off into forgetfulness, a fear seized my body. I bolted up in bed suddenly.

And he was there, standing across the room.

"Good morning." He was wearing his typical evening attire but looked freshly showered and shaved. "Where have you been?"

I could barely breathe I was so frightened, but I forced myself to calm down. After several seconds, I looked up at him again.

"Looking for Daniel Edmonds," I said.

"Who are you talking about?" he replied quickly.

"I know who you are." I was smiling now. "You killed those two men, didn't you?"

"Maybe I knew them, but the pool is open to all Adams House residents." He crossed from the doorway to my desk. He knew what I was talking about, but he wasn't acting like someone who had had his cover blown.

"How did you die? Too much to drink?" My chest was pounding but I tried to remain still.

He pointed at a half-empty bottle of tequila on my bureau. "I think the real drinker here is you, my friend. And too much if you ask me."

"I don't care who you are or what happened to you in this hellish house." I was infuriated by his aloofness, by my growing sense that nothing could be solved by this. "Why are you bothering me now?"

He gave me a bored look and nonchalantly glanced over the room, his eyes finally resting on the bathroom and the hallway. "Have the police found your friend yet?"

I could barely keep my anger in check. "Why did you kill her? Why did you kill those two classmates of yours?"

"If you really must know, look in your heart. See what lurks there. A common beat dying in each man."

"You can't do this again. You can't pin this on me." I was flailing. I had to stay clear of his half-truths.

"Dead men tell no tales, friend, and I can only talk with some knowledge about Daniel Edmonds. Then again, the whole house knew it." He brushed by my computer keyboard, hesitating for a moment, and then tapped a couple of keys querulously. "Do you realize how much harassment I got? That they got? It was a problem for many nasty people. At best, they were just ignored and resented."

I thought of the three jacks in the card deck. "Then why are you harassing me?"

He turned from my desk and window and was looking straight at me again. His skin was oily and pallid. His fiendish, black eyes were dilated to the point of having no whites to them. I must have stared into them for several seconds before he spoke again. "What if I told you that I am Maeve."

"You killed her. There's a difference."

He stepped forward. "What if I told you that Daniel Edmonds was attracted to you."

I tried to move off the bed but my overmedicated arms and legs weighed me down. My head spun, the room following its orbit. I fell back on the bed, grabbing my head with my hands.

"Just leave me alone," I screamed.

He came to the edge of the bed. "Rest and don't worry about a thing. You didn't kill Maeve and I'm no longer going to bother you."

That said, he smiled and stooped down to my bedside. A black, menacing vein popped from his forehead as he descended toward me. I tried to move away but my body was numb and removed from me—I was frozen in his gaze and my chest, arms, and legs were floating aimlessly like balloons.

"You remind me of Rockland."

The room was twirling wildly except for a single point which was him. His mad eyes still fixed and pierced through me. The vein in his forehead pooled out in utter darkness across his face like an eclipse of the moon. He bent closer down towards me. His foul breath was hot against my cheek.

"Do you love them?" he asked. He paused only for a slight moment, knowing no answer would come from me. I was helpless and held mute. Then he kissed me on the lips.

At first his lips exuded a warmth that spread quickly through my whole body. For a brief moment, my fever broke and I felt healthy and strong. What was happening? What new and old, sick thing was I becoming? I was completely passive and couldn't focus on anything but the warmth passing through me. I felt like a swooning drunk or someone trying to walk straight after riding a merry-go-round. I strained for reason. I lacked all control.

Then he moved back from me and started to laugh. It was a horrible laugh that echoed the howling I had heard the night that Maeve died. I turned away from him and the warm feeling grew into a chill. My heart was beating fast and my breath quickened, drawing short and tight. His laugh bellowed inside my head. The chill turned into a deathly cold. As I brought my arms around myself for warmth, I felt my flesh harden and desiccate. The room instantly stopped spinning. I looked down at my body, which was putrefied and decaying into my hands and before my eyes. I felt a strange numbness like needle pricks followed by a fierce coldness wrapping around my body. Dry, fetid holes eroded through my chest and legs. Skin and hair fell from my face to the mattress and floor in loathsome, rotten clumps. I tried to scream but all noise was drowned by his horrifying laugh.

I woke up in that scream, sweat dripping from every pore. The only sound in the room was the steam hissing as it pushed through the radiator coils.

He was gone.

Chapter 20

I remained awake the rest of the morning, too frightened and too tired to sleep. There was something morbid about my last encounter with him. It wasn't his control over me. It was my inability to control myself. Something had shifted. I had felt death as if it were my own.

And death was no longer a far-fetched nightmare. There was a great deal wrong with me. I was continually coughing and unable to catch my breath. My fever was running so high that I opened all the windows in the room, allowing the freezing air to burrow in. My eyesight would blur in and out, sometimes even contracting to tunnel vision. Medicine had only a minor doping effect. I was getting used to the symptoms, but the virus was wearing me thin.

I couldn't understand why he hadn't betrayed himself

or given more of a reaction when I said his name. He was either playing it cool or I was playing into what he wanted. The encounter had left me exhausted and furious. What did I know of Daniel Edmonds that didn't cloud like some dream or warped fantasy? I couldn't pull myself from the mire of fear and shame. I didn't understand—each part of my mind was suspicious of the other.

I walked across the room and emptied the pockets of my coat. I eventually found the page I had torn from the facebook. I stared long and hard at that picture of Daniel Edmonds. There was something wrong with how he looked. He had softer features in the picture—he was rounder in the face, not as gaunt in the jaw or as beetle-eyed. Then again the photo had probably been taken in his last year of high school, four years prior to his supposed death. I knew my looks had changed that dramatically over time. But the smile was different, too genuine.

I crumpled the photo in anger. A moment later I had smoothed the paper back out. It was all I had now. But even this picture told me nothing. He told me nothing. Nothing that would help me.

But I still had some vision of him. I had a very real feeling that I was close. The picture—old, young, or too happy—was a likeness, and it served as evidence that this wasn't all just inside my head. What I did know was this—he had recognized the name Daniel Edmonds. He even seemed to claim it as his name. He also knew about the drownings.

It didn't make any sense. His past had little to nothing to do with me. His tricks were maddening and I hadn't a clue what to do. I just wanted to hide and have it go away. Why hadn't the police come to interview me about Maeve? Did they even suspect me?

I had to stop him. But deep within myself, I felt his power overwhelm me. The longer I stared at the photo, the sicker I became.

I huddled silently in my dark room as the afternoon carried on in a gray sleep. Above all my fears, I was exhausted and in pain. From time to time, I drifted and jumbled over thoughts of going home and leaving school. Such escapes passed quickly as I thought of Maeve's death. When and if they found her body, I knew they would discover some lead to me. I was bound to her in death. Bound by him.

In the midst of this mess, I did manage to conjure up one bleary thought that led me on. I desperately needed to get a grasp on reality—I had to find more evidence like the picture in the facebook. I had to double-check my deranged memory with an accurate history of what happened. I had to bridge 1946 with my increasing dementia. If I could confirm the events surrounding Daniel Edmonds's death, then I could play against them. There had to be a trail left. And if I knew what was going to happen, I could avoid it. My plan was tenuous and compulsive, but I felt at the time that getting to him would exonerate me and erase my ties to Maeve's death.

There was no fate to this. No fate, I hoped.

Why didn't I just run? Something—intuition, indecision, or bloodlust maybe—was snaring me in. I didn't care about Maeve or myself anymore. I had to find out what Daniel Edmonds was after. I had to break the burning wheel and free myself. At the time, I couldn't see the repetitions—déjà vu had failed me and fate had weaved its decided way.

• • •

Barely able to get out of bed, I dressed slowly and left Adams House. I crossed Mass Ave and crept into the back entrance of Widener Library. I returned to the periodicals stacks. I decided that it was time to try the *Boston Globe* archives for more details on the drownings. The *Globe* was kept on microfilm. I found the small, black reel for November 1946 and placed it under the machine. The film was badly scratched and in horrible condition, but eventually I did find a report on the drownings. The details were similar, except no names were mentioned. The difference was puzzling, but I could understand how the College would have asked that the names be withheld. Within the tail of the story was the name of the campus security guard who initially found the three. I followed the story through its jump to the Local section. There were two photos on the page—one of the staircase and Bow Street side of B-entry and a smudged-out photo of the security guard standing on the steps in front of Westmorely Court. It was hard to say for certain, but I judged he was no older than thirty at the time. His name was Patrick Hurley.

I left periodicals and headed for the phone books in the main reading room. My legs were sore and I was shaking with weariness. I crept past the padded leather doors of the reading room. The room was fairly full and there was a severe, depressing silence to the place. A pang of guilt went through me as I mulled and fretted over my abandoned course work.

I walked as quietly as I could across the reading room. I was met by a series of quick glances followed by longer, contemptuous stares. What a sight I must have been for those studying little idiots. I hadn't bathed or shaved, even after meeting with Donahue. The semester had started so long ago it seemed. And here I was—a spook, a fright to those competitive, regurgitating bastards.

I made my way to the Boston phone books and looked up Patrick Hurley. Granted it was a long shot. If he was alive he'd be in his seventies, and there was no guarantee he hadn't retired to Florida. Nonetheless, there were three listings under the name—one in Charlestown, one in South Boston, and the last in Somerville. Somerville was the closest of the three addresses. I walked back out of the reading room. I noticed Michael in the far corner hovering over his books. There was someone else at his table. Was that Rosie? Whoever it was had her back turned to me. Michael did not look up, but he was whispering and smiling. I passed by trying not to stir his attention. I left Widener to begin my search for the Patrick Hurley who resided at 33 Creighton Street.

On a map, Somerville stretches out over Cambridge like the lobes of a liver resting sidelong a stomach. It is more suburban, more working-class, and a world away from the red bricks and historic lampposts of Boston and Cambridge. Creighton Street was about a twenty-minute walk from the Yard. This new lead gave me a burst of nervous energy and I started out anxiously. I followed along Mass Ave past Porter Square. Creighton Street was crammed with two rows of dilapidated walk-ups. The block ran a fatigued spit of earth between Mass Ave and the commuter train tracks. Number 33 was the last house on the left.

The house was a dark brown with white trim. The porch sagged like an open mouth, the front windows dark, reflective eyes. I stopped at the gate and looked up the driveway for any signs of life. The barking of a television could be heard from the street, but all the lights on the first and second floor were out. The third-floor window was backlit blue by the glow of the television.

I passed through the gate and walked up onto the porch. The floorboards creaked heavily as I walked across them. A gray cat darted from behind some hedges and then disappeared again. I found "Hurley—3A" on the mailboxes. For a moment I was ready to turn back and forget the whole thing. But I had to know, I had to have an outlet for this fear that was building up inside of me. So I settled down, coughing three or four times to clear myself out, and rang his doorbell. After several minutes, a weathered old man in a T-shirt and blue pants opened the front door and glared at me through the screen.

"Yes?"

"Hi. Are you Patrick Hurley?"

"Who wants to know?"

"I do, sir. I have some questions for you about Adams House."

"Yeah, well, I don't work at the College any more."

It was him, a single stroke of luck. I thought back to the picture of him from so long ago. I noticed that his right hand was severely atrophied and the arm was cradled birdlike against his stomach. I recalled that in the photo he had turned one-quarter away to hide his handicap.

"I understand that, but I have a question about something that happened in 1946. It happened in the pool."

"I wasn't working at Adams House then." The screen door creaked back and forth.

"But you were the one who found the three men who drowned in the pool."

"That was a long time ago." He tried to close the door.

"Please, sir, I just have a few questions. I'm doing a paper on it."

"What?"

"Yeah, I'm tracing the history of Adams House."

"Such bullshit they let you college students get away with. To hell with the College and to hell with Adams House."

"I agree. I live there."

"Yeah, you look like it." His eyes darted up and down as he looked me over.

"Could I please ask you a few questions?"

He opened the screen door and led me up the narrow staircase to the third floor. We entered the musty apartment. He had the heat on full blast. Stepping into the room was like walking towards a furnace. The television was blaring the sports update. He hobbled across the room and turned it off. There was an old wrought-iron sewing machine in the middle of the floor with a gray pant leg stretched across it. He came back through the room into the small kitchen carved out by the doorway. It looked cramped and well lived in. The weak incandescent lighting brought out the browns and yellows in the furniture and the chipping plastered walls. The oil paintings on each of the far walls had long since faded, their landscapes blurred out of spring or summer. It was a shabby, dank place.

"You want some tea?"

"Yes, thanks." I needed a rest after the walk and leaned my sore body against the end of the couch.

"You don't look too good, kid."

"I have a bit of a cold."

"Looks fatal." He laughed to himself and put the kettle on. When the tea was ready, he took his cup, gave another to me, and sat down behind the sewing machine.

"What do you want to know?"

"Did you find the three that drowned?"

"Yeah. It was dreadful. The two of them stuck together by rigor mortis, the third at the bottom of the pool. I was just back from the war. With my arm here, night watchman was about the only work I could get. I asked for a new watch after the whole thing."

"Why?"

"For one thing, there's something wrong with the place, especially that entry and courtyard around the pool." He examined the hole he was patching in the pant leg. "They said that when they dug out that pool in the thirties they found some things down there."

"Like what?"

"I don't know, it was just rumors and stories," he said, sipping tea too hot to drink.

"Did they find a mass grave?"

"No." He looked away dismissively. "No crap like that. The story was that when they were digging down they accidentally hit a steam pipe. The pipes were so old that they had rusted into the dirt, and when the pipe broke the water turned a thick red color."

"Like a pool of blood?" I sat up in my seat, thinking of my laundry.

"Yeah, something like that. Apparently it spooked the construction guys. Even after they fixed the pipes, a lot of them wouldn't work in that basin. By the end of the day it was like you were covered in blood."

"So how did the three of them drown?"

He put down his tea and ran his left hand over the sewing machine. "The first two committed suicide.

Their wrists were slashed. I could never figure out what the third guy was up to. They said he was drunk and tried to save them, but I don't know."

"Did you know any of them before they died?"

"No, but I had seen them around the house and I can tell you they were a bunch of three-dollar bills. I remember when the other cops showed up on the scene to clean the place up they started calling them the three fairies or the three Ophelias or some shit like that." He paused for a second. "The two who committed suicide were, you know, naked."

"Do you think the third guy killed them?" I asked, dreading the answer.

He took another sip from his tea, trying to put space between himself and his last comment. "I can't say. It was a long time ago. But I don't see how he could have killed both of them. The coroner speculated that the third guy drowned a while after the other two. This led everyone to believe he had come upon the scene later and was careless. Still, I had my suspicions. I can't even remember why."

His story fit the details well, but I still had very little in terms of motive. I looked for the first time at the deep cracks and fissures in his tired old face. His whole body slumped in the chair. I imagined the time and pain it took to wear a person down like that. For the moment, Patrick Hurley was my bridge between now and then.

"Are you sure you didn't know the third guy at all before he died?"

"I knew him a little. I used to see him wandering the halls and tunnels at night. Lonely guy . . ." He looked over at me suspiciously as if he had just realized that I was not taking notes.

I finished the dregs of my tea. I had to get out of there. "Thanks very much. This confirms the stories I've read."

He seemed to dismiss whatever was troubling him and grinned, showing his crooked, smoke-stained teeth. "No problem, but I don't know why you need me to retell it. No one except the police has ever asked me about it. Hard to imagine that I've been retired for fifteen years."

I turned to the door and then stopped. "Did anything else weird or unusual happen at Adams while you were there?"

"Nope. If I hadn't come upon the drownings in the pool, I might not have even known about them. Word about that stuff didn't get around much. The dean and the families of the kids were embarrassed by it and made us keep a lid on it." He pulled himself and his chair closer to the sewing machine.

"Did they pay you?"

He ran the pant leg through the sewing machine, setting the stitch with his left hand and working the needle with the foot treadle beneath the table. He brought his crippled right arm down on the table to hold everything steady. "You can't put this in your paper, but bribes were a customary part of these scandals."

"Scandals? What other scandals were there bribes for?"

"I heard from the guy who replaced me at Adams that he got fifty more than I did."

"For what?"

"For keeping quiet." His eyes widened in a familiar way and I sensed that I was wearing out my welcome.

"But what happened that he had to take that hush money?"

"A couple years later some kid in Adams House killed a girl he'd been going with." He stood up from the sewing machine.

"When?"

"I don't know. My watch was at the law library by then. I told you, it was a long time ago."

"But a couple years after the drownings?"

"One or two years, I think. Around Thanksgiving."

I started to cough loudly and tried to swallow the pain down into my chest. He came towards me.

"You should see someone about that cold. You look like a ghost."

"Yeah, I will."

He led me to the door, where I thanked him. I even promised him a copy of the paper when it was finished. He smiled and let the screen door creak closed. As I turned off Creighton Street I heard a train scream by the disused backlots. There was no one else on the sidewalk. As the train whistled into the distance, I was back on Mass Ave heading towards the College.

On my way back to Adams, I came upon the newsstand in the Square. I stopped to scan the papers. The *Globe* had a column down the front of the Metro section with Maeve's picture. Again it was her photo from the freshman facebook—her hair was longer, her face rosy like a cherub's. The picture was much clearer and she looked much younger, happier. The story reported no new leads on her disappearance and requested that anyone with information contact the police. I skipped down a few paragraphs to the quotes from the police and administration—either the cops couldn't catch a cold or they were waiting for me to slip up somehow and lead them to her.

I was puzzled and terrified by Patrick Hurley's story about the murder of the girl a few years after Daniel Edmonds's death. It could have just been rumors that ran together and were muddled over the years, but I still felt uneasy about it. I wanted to go back to my room and rest, but instead I turned sharply from the Square back into the Yard. Entering the gates, I walked by Straus Hall. I remembered when I stole a kiss from Rosie on those steps our freshman year. It was the greatest thing to love someone like that—to love her without knowing much about her, to love her without care for yesterday or tomorrow.

Now it was all coming back to haunt me. I turned into the long afternoon shadows of Matthews and Grays halls. Under the giant oaks and maples of the Yard, the air smelled like rain. For good or bad, I would be leaving this place behind soon. Twinges of regret, mostly heartbreak, and now the base fear of getting caught. Every lamppost and kiosk in the Yard was still papered with Xeroxed photos of Maeve. I had had many chances and this is what had happened. I couldn't bear to look at her image anymore.

I ducked into Widener Library and headed back up the long staircase to the periodicals archive, where I pulled down the 1947–48 volume of the College daily. I searched the entire year carefully but found no significant mention of suicide, murder, or Adams House. Maybe Hurley didn't have the story straight or had given me the wrong year.

Part of me didn't want to find out. But I had to know, I had to understand what I was up against. I went over to the *Boston Globe* archive just to see if they had picked the trash for any stories that the College had swept clean. Nothing for 1947 or 1948.

I relaxed a little at that point. I didn't want to find someone else responsible. I knew Daniel Edmonds was the root of my problems and Maeve's murder. But I was curious as to what this all meant for me. The pieces of history did not add up to anything provable. What scared me was that the facts were the same and I was sliding helplessly away from them. As foolish as it may seem now, I felt that history was supposed to fall into a certain pattern, and that knowing that pattern was enough. A loss of control, a repeat of history—I thought these were knowable items, like some silly game of trivia. Sure I was afraid of losing that game, but at the time, I was still hoping for some answers to my questions.

Maybe I was looking too hard for truth and settled for what made little sense to anyone but myself. I was desperate to find a way out, to break open my own story. I didn't want to be half the person I was capable of being. I wanted to have potential. I wanted to be smarter than the rest of them.

I walked out of the periodicals room and started to leave. I was walking down to the basement to exit onto Mass Ave when I thought about the College archive. There were alumni records down there—that would be the place to look. But to return to the scene of the fire like that? It was risky, even if I was an unknowing participant.

I left Widener and walked over to Houghton. I showed my ID at the desk. The security guard looked at it, then stared at me doubtingly. The resemblance was beginning to fade. But he let me go, and I rode the slow, wobbly elevator down to its lowest floor.

The fluorescent lights of the archive still burned bright and pale. I crossed over to the movable stacks. The far end of the stacks was covered with a tarp and police line. I saw no one else on the floor. I could hear the water pipes gurgling through the walls. I thought of the steam tunnels. With each step towards the end of the stacks, I could feel the tunnels—the very earth below me—breathing, seeping forth.

I ducked behind the tarp. The air was heavy with the smell of soot. The movable stacks had been pried open at the end. The button mechanism was smashed and in pieces. I took cautious steps, constantly looking over my shoulder. Then I peered at the ceiling, the asbestos tiles showing brown water marks.

I entered Z stacks. Two of the five sections were in cinders. If I took another step I would leave my footprint in the ash and burned carpet. I had to get over it and to the other end of the stacks where the remaining contents of Z stacks were kept.

I came back out of the row, crossed the short aisle, and grabbed three books from another section. I went back to Z stacks and carefully placed the first book down in the soot. I took a step on top of it and laid down the next book. I got across.

On the far end of Z stacks I searched the three remaining sections for anything on the years following 1946. There was little—some old graduation photos, a class song censored by the dean, but nothing compared to the bulging and overflowing files for the sixties and seventies when the students were prone to riot and Communism.

I heard footsteps. I hunched down and held my breath. The steps were coming toward me, then shuffled to a stop. I waited. I heard the slightest sound of a spring. The person—the idiot—was trying to open the movable shelves. The footsteps tramped off a few moments later. Probably some snotnose honors student who would raise hell to get a source for his moronic thesis. I had to get out of there before he came back with a librarian.

I skipped back over my book bridge and had started to walk out of the row when I noticed a stack of black-and-red books each the size of a tabloid newspaper. The books had recently been rebound, and their newness stuck out amidst the incinerated shelves. I checked one of the spines and found that they were past issues of the *Cambridge Monitor*. With the thousands of rare books crumbling to dust in the College libraries I couldn't believe they would rebind these old tabloids. And why were they in Z stacks? The series began in the twenties and ended in 1973. I picked up the volume for 1947.

It was a small local paper with mostly news of swap meets and changes in church schedules. But it was the reports ginned from the police blotter that caught my eye. The reports appeared erratically—every two or three days, but sometimes more than a week apart.

I placed the book under my arm and snuck out of the movable stacks and from behind the tarp and tape. I scooted across the floor to a study carrel. I sat down and after scanning for anyone following me, I searched each day of 1947—through every drunk arrest, kitchen fire, and burglary. There had to be a reason that those books were there.

And then I found what I was looking for. On November 25, 1947, this report was filed:

> In an unexplained double murder and suicide, college senior John Edmonds threw his girlfriend Clare Penthim four stories from the roof of Adams House and then jumped himself.
>
> Later, when police investigators entered Edmonds's dorm room they discovered a second victim, a young woman, also believed to have been murdered by Edmonds.
>
> The detectives on the scene state that Edmonds's room was a gruesome murder site. The walls were covered in blood and the woman was chained to the main room's radiator. Her body had been badly burned and was soaked in bleach to cover the stench of putrefaction.
>
> The woman, whose name was not released, was a

> known solicitor of prostitution in the Central Square area. Police say the woman worked out of a Prospect Street club, the Mousetrap.
>
> What appears to have happened, sources close to the preliminary investigation say, is that Penthim walked in on Edmonds in the process of mutilating the body of the prostitute. In a bloodlust and rage he struck Penthim. After rendering her unconscious, Edmonds dragged Penthim to the roof . . .

The report jumped to the back page. Accompanying the rest of the article were pictures of John Edmonds and Clare Penthim. My heart was racing and I stood up from my seat. A furious static of white noise began building in my ears and head. The last line of the article read:

> John Edmonds was the younger brother of Daniel Edmonds, who drowned in the Adams House pool last year.

A cold sweat broke out across my neck and back and I nearly fainted with fear. It was him—the picture of John Edmonds was exact down to those dark, catching eyes. I stepped back from the carrel, my hands and arms shaking under the weight of the book. In the rise of panic, I began to understand the mistakes I had been making—the similarities to his brother in looks, why I was being driven mad figuring out false connections. I dropped the book, which fell to the floor still open to the pictures. I began to whimper helplessly and banged into a cart, knocking over piles of unshelved books. How stupid I had been. He knew it too. That's why he was playing along and laughing at me. It was like looking in a distorted mirror and then turning away to find the whole world the same way.

I began to wail and scream in frustration. A librarian came out of the foyer for the elevators to see what was wrong. My screams died in a fit of coughing. She looked very frightened as I sneered at her. She was about to reach out to silence me, thought better of it, and then backed away to get help. When she turned around, I picked up the 1947 volume of the *Monitor* and ran out the back stairwell of the archives. I raced up three floors, my footfalls resounding through the stairwell.

I came out into a series of stuffy reading rooms for rare books—the inner cages, as they were called. I staggered past several professors, who raised their eyes from magnifying glasses ready to scold me for disturbing the silence and then refrained.

I bounced through a set of double doors. I had made it to the lobby. The security guard had his back turned from the entrance as he flirted with a checkout girl. The elevator light pinged. It would be the librarian I had seen on the archives floor. The guard started to turn. I went for it and sped by the bag checker and out of the library's entrance, and didn't stop until I reached Mass Ave.

I was dripping with sweat and could feel a fever running up my back into my neck and head in a series of devastating chills. I should have read over the story again. I should have gotten the details straight. As I ran across the traffic on Mass Ave, I tasted something strange, and when I raised my hand to my mouth, my fingers drew blood. I had bitten through my tongue. The brown evening skies started to spit icy rain.

I finally stumbled down Mass Ave and along the curve of Bow Street to the B-entry doors. I stood there for a moment catching my breath and swallowing the blood in my mouth. I had a vision of a wave of blood rising out of the Adams House pool and flooding the ground floor. I saw the bodies of those who had been murdered bobbing like broken mannequins. The viscous tide and wake of the blood washed over me, its dark red film sticking to the walls and pouring off my face like wine cascading down the side of a glass.

I kept swallowing the blood that seeped from my tongue and headed up the stairs. As I climbed to the second floor I heard a slight echo of laughter coming from outside. On the third-floor landing I looked into the courtyard, which was lit with strings of Chinese paper lamps. The music and laughter crept on, growing in volume. Lightning blazed suddenly over the courtyard and I could make out over a dozen shadows of people caught in that split of light. The rain now was pouring in thick drops and I couldn't understand what this party was for. Another flash of lightning and the music, the lamps, and the shadowy figures had vanished. I staggered away from the window as the rain splattered against it. A thunderclap boomed down and rolled over the house, startling me out of the wash of this mirage.

I reached the fourth floor and opened the door to my room. I was thoroughly exhausted and needed to splash myself with cold water. I took off my coat and turned to the bathroom door. The room was filthy and reminded me of the old man's apartment. The brass knob of the door was covered in dried blood. I was furious at myself for having overlooked the blood there for all this time. I pushed the bathroom door open to get a towel and some cleaner.

Lying there in a tub full of bleach was Maeve's tattered and disfigured body.

• • •

I backed out into the main room and tripped over the doorsill, crashing headfirst to the floor. As my vision came out of blurriness, I noticed from across the floor that the radiator was smeared with blood. Wrapped around the coils were pieces of rope tied on one end and torn on the other. I raised my head and found the mattress slowly dripping red drops like a soaked sponge. The radiator began to hiss and clank, the metal pipes stretching and gurgling up and down the wall of the room. I tried to scream but my mouth was too dry and clotted with blood.

I got to my knees and crawled to the bathroom to stop the bleeding in my mouth. The smell of bleach reached my nose again and I scurried away like a hurt animal. The look of horror on Maeve's face was scored into my memory. The burns ripped through her soft skin; her eyes sunken into the stare of death. All this blood was hers. I began to cry hysterically and fell back against the bedposts and the floor.

I must have passed out at that point and from there fell further into a deep sleep. What came then was almost inevitable. I dreamt I was back on the fourth floor of Matthews, back in that cold, dark room. For so long I had tried to forget. So long I've been stuck in this past.

I was walking from the bedroom to the bathroom just as I did that first night of spring break and the countless times I have remembered it since. I was even singing softly to myself. *This heavy heart I carry.* There was some candlelight coming from behind the bathroom door. And as I entered the bathroom I saw a small yellow candle on the sink.

But that's not what I saw first. That was just a stupid

little detail that tries to keep some distance from that night. Why couldn't I remove myself from this repetition? Why the endless, inevitable déjà vu?

What I saw first was Billy hanging from the shower curtain rod. Startled, I bumped the door wide open and stumbled back into the hallway. But my numbness gave way to a surge of fear. His head was sunk into his chest and he was slowly swaying from side to side. A scream shot out of me uncontrollably and my hands trembled in terror.

And then Billy raised his head up and looked at me.

His eyes. How could I forget? His eyes shimmering in fear. His face a dark crimson flush with veins bulging across his forehead. Why? Because of Rosie and me. He tried to open his mouth, but all I heard was his sputtering choked-off breath.

I took a tentative step towards him. I was completely terrified. Billy started kicking and convulsing. And his eyes—swelling horribly now, the rims tearing in the pale yellow light. Billy raised his arm, jerking it toward himself.

He was asking me to help him. But I didn't move. Something, envy maybe, wouldn't let me go.

And then there was a knock at the door. I froze, staring at Billy's anguish. I don't why. I don't know what happened to me. I was part panic-stricken, but there was some depraved fascination reeling within me. I felt some sick joy in the fact I had driven him to it. But that's not it. That's not why. That was all after the fact. We have no reasons. We just stop, go, help, hurt.

I stepped past Billy and over to the bathroom window. Another knock at the door, louder and more impatient. I turned back to look at Billy and caught my reflection in the mirror over the sink.

The candlelight was very dim, but what I saw in that

mirror horrified me. The reflection was not my own. It was Edmonds, and he knew. He knew I was looking through my eyes at him. He looked confident and gave himself a wry smile. It was him, I swear. And I could feel him deep inside me, studying my every thought. Poor pitiful me. School was too much pressure. Betrayed by friends. Can't blame anyone but myself. I had set my own traps. One vague and despairing thought after another, and he knew them all.

Billy's choking had reached a cruel and sickening point. Each breath now seemed like a hoarse whisper that carried my name. I wanted to reach out and help, but it felt too late. Another series of knocks and then someone banging the door against the chair propped against it. I turned to face Billy one last time, but his head had fallen again. He who hesitates is lost. He had stopped kicking. I turned back toward the window. His poor, dangling body; his closeness to death overpowering and confusing. He was no longer trying to breathe. I again saw myself in the mirror. The reflection was my own. Scared and witless me.

I crawled out onto the fire escape and closed the window behind me. Someone was calling out hello from inside the room. I couldn't look back. It was freezing outside, and the numbness quickly returned. I was leaving him behind. It wasn't my fault. He couldn't have known. Each step was braced now with the fear of getting caught. But what did I do? I couldn't reason it out. I could only run like some child trapped inside his own nightmares. I quickly scampered down the three flights of the fire escape and fell hard into the bushes behind Matthews Hall. Although it was spring break, I could hear laughter coming across the courtyard and heading my way. I couldn't be seen in the Yard. I ran back into Matthews and darted down the stairs to the basement.

I made my way through the laundry room and down a dingy corridor to the boiler room. Still I could hear footsteps. And laughter. Laughter trickling through the air and down to the basement. Laughter always following me.

Behind the boiler was a large black door. It seemed to be bolted shut, but when I turned the knob the door opened easily. I heard screams coming from above. Only later did I find out that this was Rosie.

I spun through the door and slammed it shut. The numbness in my arms and legs tingled away, leaving only the brutal pain of having utterly failed Billy. I took a few steps down a pitch-black hallway, finally coming to a long, descending staircase illuminated by a series of dim lightbulbs. Down I went, trying to get as far from Billy as possible. With each step down, the air grew warmer and more humid. Billy had ended something and I was not one to interfere. Then again, I had failed the hardest test of my life. With each step, I was becoming more and more a failure. College was irrelevant. I had sidestepped the most basic, decent thing to do. And with it, grew this void—a void of disgust, pity, and paranoia.

When the stairwell ended, I found myself inside the old steam tunnels. I stopped to catch my breath amid the stifling air. I closed my eyes for a few moments trying to gather myself. But the only thing I could summon was a constant replay of Billy's tortured face as he reached out to me. I started to cry. His eyes, so tired of fighting, and so aware of what I had done to him. Why hadn't I helped him? Why had I pushed him to it?

I heard a door above me open. They were on to me fast. Someone must have seen me on the fire escape. I heard footsteps. I ran frantically through the tunnel. But it was my guilt that was chasing me. As I went faster, the footsteps began to trail off, and then all I could hear was my own wheezing breath, a sound that reminded me of Billy's last aggravated gasps. I ran and ran until I came to another door. It was dark, but I found the latch and tried to open it. It was stuck. I pushed and pulled but it would not give. Then I felt something warm and syrupy drip over my hand. I stood back and watched the door ooze with dark blood. I screamed as the blood dribbled down, pooling in front of me. I ran on, again hearing footsteps behind me. Footsteps and a deep murmur of voices. I came to a fork in the tunnels. I turned left and after a short, uphill run came to another door. I tried the knob quickly. Locked. The door was wood and had partially rotted away. I pressed against it, but it held. The distant voices grew louder. A flashlight was shimmering across the point at which I turned. I was trapped in a maze of shadows and echoes. A maze of my own fear and the wish that I hadn't ran. I took a few steps back and ran at the door. I just had to break free of Billy. I had to start over. I hit the door at full speed. The door began to give and I felt a tremendous suction pulling me as I kicked through the rotten wood. The door flew open and instantly I was blinded by the most intense sunshine.

And I was outside. It was the middle of the day and I staggered out into the light. The echoes of the tunnel panned into outdoor crowd noises. I took a couple more steps and fell over a folding chair. As I got up my eyes were finally coming into focus, and in front of me I could make out Apthorp House and its courtyard. I could barely see and I was breathing hard from running through the tunnels. I heard scores of people chattering away.

More laughter, more voices. I had adjusted to the brightness when I found myself standing just a few feet from my mother and father. They were dressed nicely and were seated on the lawn in folding chairs. And they were among hundreds of other parents—prim and attentive, all looking for that certain, special someone.

It was graduation.

A band began to play. Pomp and circumstance. A procession into the courtyard began and everyone in the senior class was wearing their caps and gowns. Everyone but me. I saw the master of the house making his way through the graduates and I moved toward him. I was a few feet away from him, but the closer I got, the harder it became to pull through the crowd and reach him. He walked behind Apthorp House and disappeared. The swarms of people congratulating each other made it impossible for me to pass through.

That's when I heard a familiar voice from behind. I turned around and there was John Edmonds standing in the middle of the courtyard and laughing at me. He was wearing a cap and gown. He moved a step toward me, and as his gown moved in the light I realized it was covered in blood. He pointed and everyone looked at me. I shied away from their faces and stuck my head into my chest. I looked down to find my hands were covered in blood. I panicked and quickly looked back up at the crowd. They all had begun to laugh at me now and I couldn't stand it. I tried to cover my ears with my hands but they dripped with blood. I couldn't hide my hands or myself from them. I couldn't make them stop. Their mocking laughs echoed horribly through my fragile sleep.

I awoke what felt like days later to the taste of dried blood on my lips and tongue. My dreams had been dreadful and grim and I was more exhausted than before I had fallen into sleep. My body had just about given out. My fever was gone, but I was unable to keep myself warm. I was cold and alone.

I was clouded in the first waking thoughts of where I was. Then I looked around the room—the trail of blood from the radiator to the bathroom, the burned sheets in the fireplace, Maeve, lifeless and inbrined in a tub of bleach—and the fear came back to me in one great rush. I had been tricked and betrayed. I had sleepwalked into murder. Had I really done this? How could I have done this? No, he was the murderer.

It wasn't my fault. I had been baited. Now I had to coax him out and sidestep the blame. I would always have my questions, and he would always have his vague replies, but that didn't matter now. I didn't care anymore about the toll on my life this had taken. I was past the point of caring about anything or anyone—except, of course, John Edmonds. And I had to erase him from my history.

This is where the end begins.

I jumped out of bed and looked one more time into the bathroom. Maeve still lay preserved in the blood-streaked tub, a shrine of my own guilt. The expression on her face seemed more tortured than before. I still could not believe that I was blinded to all of this. Blinded by him.

My heart beat fast and I took panicked gasps for air. I thought over the whole night I last saw Maeve. There was a clear chain of events in which he was the murderer. I was muddled by my own petty fear. And he was the catalyst of that fear. I just had to sort out my details, what I was doing that night. But how could he possibly have brought her body up the stairs without anyone seeing? I needed an alibi that placed me away from my own room. How was any of this possible? How could I have any hope? How could I have done this?

"She must have come willingly to your room that night."

There he was. John Edmonds was sitting on my bed grinning at me.

"I know you did this." I tried to concentrate on playing the role he now expected of me.

"How could I? I don't exist, remember?" He tested the rusted mattress coils on the bed. Blood seeped down the bedpost in thin rivulets to the floor. "I'm just as strong as you make me. You brought her up here after the dance, raped her, and then this." His hands curled and swept over the room like dark wings.

"I know who you are now. I know you killed those two girls." That's right, I thought, play the fool—the loud, angry idiot he wants. "Go to hell."

"If only there were such a place for the likes of you and me." He scraped a piece of dried blood from the mattress and smeared it between two fingers.

I looked away from him. Everything he said was two-faced but true: he was what I made of him. A seething anger, black and unbearable, rose in my chest. I was trapped like a stupid animal in my own suffering.

"You really don't get it," he said.

"What, that your past is my prologue? Forget it."

"You can still escape. It's not like you'll end up dead."

I looked down to avoid his eyes but still they pierced through me. I wished I were dead. And my choices were narrowing down that road. I had to stop the self-pity act, it made him too strong. I had to concentrate. I had to play him for some sort of upper hand. Conversation was futile. He could see through me, because I could see through myself. I was no longer an honors student. I was no longer special. I was an unhappy victim. I was going to be accused of murder. And he had done this to me. He who was controlled by me. It was a sick circle and my head was swimming in his presence. I could barely see straight from the energy he sapped from me.

"Death is just a state of mind now." The voice was different but familiar.

I rolled my eyes back up at him. There was Maeve in a black dress, beautiful and alluring, sitting on the bed. She was without burns or scars, but her face seemed thin, her complexion piqued. "Time ticks by very slowly in this old hall. So slowly, you'll never be able to tell." She raised her arms towards me. "Don't worry. You're a good person. So smart and handsome. Everyone likes you. And I love you."

The last few words lowered to the timbre of his voice and I was utterly terrified. I stepped away from the bed.

Again he laughed at me. I had to leave the room. As I stepped toward the door I heard a feverish, nervous voice from deep inside my head call out to me. None of this was happening. I was not a murderer. I couldn't go on, I couldn't get caught. I turned again to the bed and there now sat Rosie.

"Don't go, I'm just getting used to having you back."

I couldn't stand his antics any longer. Things I wanted to hear and he knew it. I was right to be paranoid and believe nothing. Nothing had truly happened to me that year. He had just played me for the fool and set me on problems and doubts with no answers, no solutions. No one was out to get me, except myself. Since freshman year, it was all my fault. Each and every one of those voices was from inside my head. The College experience. The old college try. They are there to help you. All of my problems were airy nothings that he teased out from my fears. God help me.

I had to get out of that room and out of the house.

I ran to the door and in a blink Rosie stood before me. "You can't leave. After all I've done for you. I love you. You must love me."

At this she put her hand out. I wanted to hold her. I wanted to be held. What had happened to all my friends? What had I done? I could feel my blood run weak as water. Tears began to stream down my face and I could barely see through them. I wanted to believe. I wanted to leave that dorm room, that school, with her. I wanted to live past this.

That's when my dreams came crashing through. I woke to Rosie's screams as she stood in the doorway to my bathroom.

I was lying with my neck resting at the bottom of the bedpost, the rest of me strewn across the floor. I must have passed out again. The room was still a bloody mess. Nothing had changed except that Rosie had barged in and ruined everything. I was startled and afraid of her. What if she went to the police? What if she brought the police with her? Thoughts of getting caught raced past me.

Then it hit me. How could I be sure this was really Rosie? Rosie stopped screaming and stumbled back into the main room.

"Oh my God."

"Rosie, please."

"You sick fuck."

"I need your help." I pulled myself up from the floor.

"Stay away from me."

Was it her? Maybe, maybe not. Her fear and shock seemed real. But so was mine, and I knew he was a part of me now. When I stood up, Rosie took quick notice that I blocked the path to the door. She tensed up, trying to think of a way around me. Now I was threatening her. But that didn't matter. I was under the wheel of all of this and couldn't see the upside coming. If it was him, who stood before me? He couldn't really do anything to me. He could only pretend. And I could test him. I also could pretend to act his fate out. And then I would catch him. I could make the past solely the past.

"What day is it?"

She ignored me and pointed to the bathroom.

"What day is it?" I yelled and stepped toward the bathroom. I slammed the door quickly in a vain attempt to remove it from her mind.

"It's November twenty-fourth." There was John Edmonds lounging on the mattress again. He was grinning at me. "You must admit the timing is impeccable."

"What do you want?" I screamed at him. Rosie continued to stare in shock at the bathroom door. She was acting as if she couldn't see or hear Edmonds. If it was Rosie, though, she had seen enough. I looked down at my shirt, which was smeared with blood from brushing against various parts of the room. There was nothing I could do to save her. I could only test him. For the first time, I had a plan that made sense. I had to set a trap. She was frightened, but I had to use her. I needed her help.

"She just came by before holiday break to pick up her remaining stuff," Edmonds said. He hopped up from the bed and shadowed Rosie as she pulled back from me. She was figuring out how to make a break for it. He meanwhile was loving every minute of this torment. "And she walks in on this."

"Leave me alone," I screamed at Edmonds, but succeeded only in further terrifying Rosie. Tears choked back her words. I was still standing between her and the door. I tried to grab her by the wrist, but she pulled away.

"I can't believe this," she said in a hopeless and cracked voice. She looked at the dried blood smeared on the walls and the mattress. Then I saw her eyes fall on the shredded rope tied to the coils of the radiator. She was piecing together what had happened and quickly realizing the danger she had stepped into.

Was she part of the illusion? I decided to try another test.

"Rosie," I asked, "did Billy know about us before he hanged himself?"

John Edmonds chuckled slightly at my question. "Come on now, that old story. We all know who drove him to suicide. Were you so jealous of Rosie having Billy that you had to betray them both? Why put all of us through your own self-deceit?" He picked up the volume of the *Cambridge Monitor* from my floor and began to flip through the pages. A thought came across his face and he looked back up at me. "Or maybe someone found Billy before he was completely dead? Was he still alive? Was he just hanging there while you watched? Maybe you helped more than anyone knows?"

He had crossed the room again and shot over his cruelest grin yet. "Maybe we should ask him."

He threw open the bathroom door. Even Rosie noticed that, I think. There was Billy hanging from the shower rod. He was clutching at the belt. He was choking and trying to stop it all from happening. Just as I remembered.

"Not much to say?" Edmonds mockingly offered Billy. "Maybe you'd like to answer the door. It's Rosie."

I heard a pounding at the door. I took my eyes off Billy and the bathroom and found Rosie had run past me. She pounded and kicked at the door, but it was locked or jammed. Something told me he would not let her go, he was keeping this illusion of Rosie here for me. He was just playing up the drama, trying to get me caught up in the pace of it. I looked back at Billy, who just glared hopelessly at me.

"So how long were you and Billy . . ." Edmonds trailed off as he circled around to the door, passed through Rosie, and then came back towards me. "Was he going to tell her?"

The pain I saw in Rosie's face said it all. The helplessness, the shame I felt. But she knew. Edmonds was right. He stepped closer to me. "No, he wasn't. He was keeping her."

Stop this. All over Rosie, for God's sake. No, that wasn't the reason. Billy's eyes were wide in fear.

"I didn't do anything to Billy," I answered in a desperate plea. "I would never kill anyone."

At that, Rosie began to scream at the top of her lungs. Her reaction was another mixed response, another half-truth adding to my confusion and torment. In the instant that she screamed, I took my eyes off John Edmonds and he had disappeared. But that didn't matter. I knew that he was trying to scare me, trying to make me do something foolish. I could catch him later that night. All of this had to be his doing. It had to be an illusion made of my own fears.

"To hell with you," I said and took another step towards her. Towards him.

She desperately tried to turn the lock. Then she pulled at the knob furiously. Would he have her run like this? I moved between her and the door and pushed her down. Her face was completely terrified. There was nothing I could do.

It must have been him. It must be him. I had to know. It had to end.

She scrambled to her knees and picked up my hammer from the desk. I moved to hit her and she stabbed the back of the hammer into my leg. Pain shot through my leg and mingled with my anger like hot tar. I grabbed her hair and dragged her to the floor. She started to scream, biting my hand as I tried to cover her mouth. I ripped up an extension cord running across the floor from the lamp to the computer. If this really was Rosie, I could still catch him; I just needed her as bait. She made one last lunge and kick to get to the door but I had wrapped the cord around her neck already. I snapped her back by the neck like a doll.

She turned and looked me in the eyes as I choked her. I still didn't know if it was really her. That fear in her eyes, that was my fear too. I was afraid of getting caught. I was afraid of death and the end of my time.

If it was John Edmonds, I would strangle him completely right then and there. But I was unsure. In the back of my mind, I worried that this was my last shot at getting back at him.

After about two minutes, she passed out completely. Her eyes fluttered into the backs of their lids. I checked her heart. It was still beating.

I went into the bathroom. Maeve was there in the tub and no one had apparently tried to move her. I then peeked out into the hall. I took a quick step into the breezeway, listened, and found all of B-entry empty. It must really have been right before Thanksgiving and I was relieved that everyone had left for the holiday. I still had a chance of catching John Edmonds without anyone catching me.

I dragged Rosie across the hallway to the base of the roof ladder. The cord was still around her neck, but I could hear her breathing. It was probably her, but that didn't matter. I had to use her as part of the trap. I went back to shut the door to my room. As I closed it, the door suddenly pulled open and there stood Maeve, her body, a rotted thing of broken tissue. She glared at me with horrible, blood-soaked eyes.

"Do it. Throw her off the roof." She spoke without moving her lips or mouth. I jumped back and almost fell over Rosie, who showed the first signs of coming to. Maeve's voice echoed and seeped through the entry and my mind like a thousand hisses and breaks of steam. When I looked up again at the door no one was there.

I lifted Rosie over my shoulder and took the ladder slowly. She was heavier than she looked and my leg was bleeding badly, the hammer having left a deep gash. For the first time in months, though, I felt strong. It was clear that this path, this whole history, had to be burned clear. I climbed the ladder to the roof quickly. I was ready for him.

I laid Rosie's body by the ledge and stopped to catch my breath. I leered over the rooftops of Cambridge so bright and comfortable during this bleak hour. The night was shrouded in low clouds. To the south and east, I could see the faintest traces of the Back Bay. The Charles was an icy, white line drawn behind the river houses and towers. The weather needle of the Hancock was bleeding red.

Rosie was still unconscious and taking short, jerky breaths for air. I loosened the extension cord even though it was no longer choking her hard. She looked like she was struggling out of a bad dream. I wasn't going to hurt her anymore. I had mistaken Rosie for his tricks, but that didn't matter. I could save the both of us now.

A group of bats fluttered out of the bell tower at St. Paul's and headed north into the weather. Seconds later, the bell struck four in the morning. He was there that instant, standing by a chimney on the far side of the roof.

He walked across the roof with a slight limp. I could see him fully after a few steps. His features seemed paper-thin, like a mask rather than a true face. He was a paltry thing, his eyes and cheeks rubbed out and pallid.

"So this is it, my old man." He lit a cigarette with my missing Zippo and offered it to me.

I took it. Was I playing along? He was about to speak when I interrupted, "Looks like we got a live one here." I started laughing and he began to smile.

"Are we waiting for anyone else?"

"Just you."

"I'm very proud of how far you've come."

"This is the only way really." I smiled and he drew nearer.

"I only wish your brother were here for this," I said.

"What?"

"Your brother, Daniel."

His smile turned to a scowl.

"I've been thinking about it. And you know . . ." I looked him right in the eye and turned us both by walking around him. We were now a few feet from the ledge. "I think you were there the night he died in the pool."

"Stop talking nonsense." He looked over at Rosie. "You know what we're here for."

"Were your brother and you very close? I mean, did you share things? Boyfriends maybe?"

"Shut up. You'll ruin this." Rosie groaned and started moving her head off her arm.

"Did he steal someone from you? Maybe Rockland Weir knows? Or was it Aaron?" I dragged heavily on the cigarette and flicked it over the edge. He knew about Billy, I knew about Daniel. "How could you kill your own brother?"

"Leave him out of this."

"Or maybe you were ashamed of him? Maybe he was your tangled mirror. I'm sure his reputation preceded you. Daniel was what you loathed about yourself."

He was ready to explode and his body expanded into the darkness. "You're the one who's a murderer. You're the one who talks to the voices in his head. Who am I? John Edmonds? Maeve? Billy? You make us all sick. You're covered in blood. You wanted them all dead." He pointed at Rosie. "There's only one way to clean up this mess and save yourself."

At this, I grabbed him by the neck and wrestled him down to the ledge. He struggled to get free but I had him pinned. I could feel him reeling into the past, passing like the shadow he was. Pure, black anger rushed through me.

And it was at that moment that I reversed my fate.

Squirming against the ledge, he stopped suddenly and smiled. I could see the blood seeping out of his mouth and down his throat. His body was as cold as mine.

"You only know what I show you," he gasped. "You never understood that."

He had preyed on me for so long. I pushed him further over the ledge. I was in danger of falling with him. He began to laugh. I thought of Billy and Maeve and in that instant they seemed two sides of the same coin. His laughter was maddening, but I could still somehow hear Rosie. I could hear her staggered breath, her strained whimpers as she came to. It was a clue that I could hear Rosie, but I ignored it. I was past the point of care and his laughter was just mocking me, mocking my trivial, fucked-up life. I had my hands clenched against his shoulders and I pushed him back as hard as I could. But he wasn't struggling. He stopped laughing and for the briefest of moments looked straight at me.

And in that moment he whispered, "Desperate and wrong—I know you will end too."

I threw him off the roof.

I woke to the toll of bells. The air smelled crisp, and I could make out a hint of sweet woodsmoke from a distant chimney. Numbness crept through every part of me. It strangely felt like I was floating.

As I began to sit up, the bells lost their harmony and came screaming in like sirens. I was lying near the roof ledge huddled by the overturned water tower. My body was stiff and bent out like a disused toy soldier. My vision was blurry and I just wanted to fall back into the hum and lilt of sleep.

This drowsy numbness was interrupted as someone lifted me to my feet. My head, full of sleep, dangled limp on my shoulders. My body was so depleted and lifeless that I was reminded of a song I had heard as a child. Something about skeletons and sacks of bones. That's what I felt like—a sack of bones. I again tasted the traces of blood in my mouth. I squinted, the view from the roof coming into form. The first blue beams of dawn rose over Boston.

I felt myself dragged a couple steps before realizing fully what was happening. I focused on the right shoulder of the man that carried me and saw the dark blue badge of a policeman. My whole body clenched and I put my feet forward, stopping both of us.

"He's awake."

"Get him some cuffs."

I coughed and shivered. I looked down and found a trail of blood drops crossed over the studs and ribs of my tuxedo shirt. I searched the ground, still in a daze. It had snowed recently and a fresh inch or so had blanketed the roof. In the corner by the water tower, a highball glass lay overturned, a thin crack running down its side. I looked back to the ledge. Several pools of blood lay smeared and frozen across the new snow.

"Get him a blanket."

I tried to raise my neck to look up but the cold had made it incredibly stiff and painful to do so. All I could see was the pools of blood and the faint, violet shadows of the policemen growing in the light of dawn. My mind swooned over the events of the night. I could hear my own heartbeat limping along. My breath seeped softly into the frozen still air. For once the roof seemed so quiet. I asked what was going on.

"You have the right to remain silent."

I still have my rights. I weakly smiled, remembering how I had thrown him over the roof. "He's silent now. And I'm free."

The cop looked over to the detective. The detective in turn gave a sideways glance to the sergeant, who was rolling yellow tape around the chimney and towards the ledge.

"Why am I being arrested when he did it?"

"Who did it?" the detective asked. He slapped on the cuffs. They were tight and cold as the air.

"John Edmonds."

"Sure he did." The voice was pedantic and familiar. I recognized Detective Reilly. "Run that name. You have the right . . ."

"You won't find anything on him, he's dead."

"Dead?" The detective grabbed me by the scruff of the neck.

"Since 1947. Look back, in the papers, the year 1947, and you'll find him." A drop of blood left my mouth and ran down my chin.

Reilly sneered at me with disgust and disbelief. He had those dark and long-jawed Irish features. His breath stank of coffee. "Okay, take him down."

"But I'm free. The house is clean," I said.

"That's enough."

As we approached the ladder to the roof, another officer appeared from below. We stopped to let him pass. I could hear Reilly behind me tapping a pen on his memo book. They never would figure it out. My arresting officer loosened his grip on me. Then he let go of me entirely and I drooped into the snow. I turned as I fell and could now see the other detectives and officers conferring. For several minutes I lay there shivering in the cold, hunched over like a beast. One of the detectives, Black, I think, strolled out on the perimeter of the roof. He wore a dark coat and fedora. He looked over the ledge and then back to the roof hatch, judging each distance. He then stepped back and conferred with one of his associates. With his back turned to me, Black looked different, familiar. An officer discreeetly asked him a question. Black turned and pointed at a spot on the roof.

Then a strange revelation came to me. With it, I was ready to throw the rest away, to forgive and to forget. I even hoped I could live through this mess. But then it happened, what I was waiting for all along. I was watching Black, when for an instant, I could have sworn that the detective looked like Billy. My dull and hazy vision had started to clear. I was woozy, but I stood up slightly to get a better look at this man. Then I realized that his dark clothes matched John Edmonds's in a way. All this time, I wanted to see through to the differences. But it was the semblances to which I was blind.

It couldn't be Edmonds, though. This man had the same short dark hair as Billy. Still with his back to me, I couldn't see the eyes and was unsure.

I peered at him for a few more moments. And just when I was certain it was Billy, the detective was called away. He walked behind the chimney towards the far side of the roof. I watched him as best I could, struggling to keep my eyes open. The other policemen appeared busy by the ledge. He walked stiffly like Edmonds. They were all so the same. All out to torture me. But I knew Billy didn't blame me. He knew I loved him. And I loved Rosie. I took care of her. Why blame me?

That's when this man looked back at me. It was Edmonds and it was Billy. They were so alike, my fear, my shame, so similar. He had me all along. But he did not smile or wince at me. His look was calm, it passed no judgment, offered no sympathy or opinion. And as he reached the far corner of the roof, he changed. Black wings, large and smooth, cast a darkness over his back.

He was still looking at me, his stare piercing through. I was transfixed by those eyes, a growing warmth burning me clean. The wings, like a shadow cast out by light, rose from his arms and shoulders, ready to soar.

And in the same instant the wings disappeared. I had blinked. It was just a man, small and cold. I guess that was the last thing my imagination had to offer. A trick of the snow's reflection and the morning light shimmering over the roof. The sun ducked behind the clouds, the darkness fluttered in. I blinked again and then stooped over to take some new snow in my hands. I felt nothing. My hands were numb. The man was gone, my soul as well.

And after all of it, I might still seem unsure. But that's not right. I knew what had happened. And what of the truth? I understood the only truth—myself. The rest was confusion, misery. The others would be as confused as those half-witted policemen were on the ledge that morning.

Exhausted, I fell to my knees. Reilly finished his notes and passed between the ladder and me. "Someone call the dean and get him over here." Then he looked at me. "What's the girl's name?"

"Who, Maeve?"

"Who do you think I'm talking about?"

"Edmonds killed her in the steam tunnels."

"Do you want to start telling the truth?"

"I prefer what happened."

Reilly shook his head and stepped away. He called over to one of the officers and told him to find my room and check it out. I peered over at the Hancock weather vane, which had turned clear blue. The clouds were breaking over the harbor and it was going to be a cold, clear, and sunny day. I looked at Reilly climbing down the ladder and then over to the ledge where the trail of blood had pooled and frozen. As the sun ascended over the ledge, I felt this tremendous sense of déjà vu. Something inside me clicked, and the wheels of the past ground finely in. Was it happening again? The illusion, these murders, this lie?

"Rosie." I could barely say her name before I started shivering like mad. He had tricked me to the end. How could I have fallen for this? We were so alike. I thought I knew him. But then, no one really knows what happened. My head began to throb deeply and I felt the rigid grasp of the cop again. I began to cry.

"No, no, no. Rosie. No. It was him!"

It *was* him. He did all of this and I could tell by their looks that they believed me. Or at least, they would understand after I explained. Someone has to believe me. I know the truth. Are they blind? Where are you, Rosie? I was lost but now am found. Why did you let Michael take you home? Billy knew. And I found out, just like he did.

I started to convulse. Two or three other policemen came rushing at me. I had rid myself of Edmonds, but at what cost I wasn't told. A pain cracked into the back of my head and came burning down into my neck and shoulders. Hands grasped and pushed at me and I fell into the snow like it was a bed of down. This was all fine now. It was all done. Here comes sleep. And this is what we want, right, John?

The last open thing I saw was the blue of the sky turn black.

At the Cambridge police station in Central Square, I gave them my story. They interrogated me for hours. I gave them my story. They didn't believe a word.

I gave them my story again. All of this, I can tell you now, has become an act. Mindless recitation. My eyes glaze over thinking about it and the words follow the actions. There's an order to the words, and I can't break myself of it now.

My parents got me a lawyer, and in preparation for the trial I had to visit this half-wit shrink. But I had already fought and lost. Did I even fight him? It was during my second meeting with the shrink that I realized this was going nowhere and there was no sense in trying.

"Did they check the yearbook for John Edmonds?" I asked.

"Yeah, he was part of that class."

"And did he murder two women?"

"He murdered a woman."

"And?"

"And he fell off the Adams House roof trying to kill a second girl." The shrink looked down at his notes. "A girl named Clare Penthim."

"She died?"

"No."

"That's not what the *Monitor* reported."

"We've been over this before. The *Cambridge Monitor* doesn't exist."

"But I stole a copy from the library."

"They didn't find any record of the paper in the library and the book they found in your room was a compilation of *Time.*"

Had Edmonds made up his own story? Was this all a fiction that I had fallen into? In a way, I guess I completed his story. In another way, I plagiarized most of it and gave it a new ending. His games made perfect sense and I still didn't understand a thing.

A couple of days into their investigation, the detectives responded to a call on Creighton Street and found Patrick Hurley hanging by an electrical cord in the shower. The coroner estimated the time of death to correlate with the day a neighbor had witnessed my visit to his house. My prints were all over a teacup and I am the only suspect.

And as for Billy. They reopened the case. But that's probably some sort of standard procedure. Take my word, they'll find nothing new. Billy and I were very secretive.

But at that point, little mattered. In my later meetings with the psychiatrists, I pulled out all the stops—urinating on myself, banging my head on tables, coming on to the orderlies, etc. I had practiced being crazy so long, it came rather naturally to me. Frankly, what difference is there?

The College covered up the affair with the convenience of Thanksgiving break. None of the papers got wind of it, and the families, my own especially, grieved quietly. I was found insane by a judge and shoved out of the way. After graduation, Susan and Michael came out with their stories—thinly veiled pieces of fantasy. Michael even claimed that Rosie was just waiting for graduation to come so she could break up with me and go off to Philadelphia with him. Philadelphia? Apparently they'd both been offered consulting jobs there and hadn't told me. Enjoy consulting the acres of burnt-out wasteland.

But by the time people started asking questions, I was long gone—expunged from the record. Which adds a level of mystery people will undoubtedly read into. But what difference does that make now? This story comes to you between doses of medication. Hours are like minutes. I'm here forever.

The funny thing is that I'm the one who's haunting the place now. I heard that my story is now legendary at Adams House and all around campus. I also heard my room was locked up or turned into a janitor's closet. It's been three years now but I guess I am still there in spirit.

I never saw him again and through this dullness I can't feel him at all. But that doesn't bother me. I know he's nearby. They tell me I'm getting better but I have to watch it or they'll send me to prison. I never graduated, of course, but what does that matter? No more progress for me; no more trying to succeed. Which is just fine, because the only thing worse than trying to succeed at that damn school was failing.

I know nothing, that much is certain. And what we do is no indication of what we think. The lies become easier and easier to live with. That's what being a person becomes: swallowing the lies you favor. Plots and errors happen and I have nothing more to say about it. You deserve it and I deserve better. Just remember how safe I am in my ignorance. You're the one with the possibilities and the problems now.

There was something about how Edmonds used my own ingrown fears against me—that's the only thing that still makes me angry. I saw it all coming and could do nothing. Try believing yourself like I did and you'll see.

Billy, Rosie, and Maeve. In you, let my true sins be remembered.

Acknowledgments

I would like to thank the following people who have helped me along the way: Anne and Daniel Desmond, David Oglesby, Richard Dowlearn, Verlyn Klinkenborg, Helen Vendler, Edwin Barber, Gerald Howard, Kristine Dahl, Lynda Obst, Alicia Gordon, Lisa Tarchak, Elizabeth and John Cordaro, Sean Fitzpatrick, and Michael Wertheim.

Special thanks to Richard Abate, a dear friend who helped me build this from an idea into a book. To Melissa Jacobs for her kind attention to every detail and keen editorial advice. And to Susan Cordaro, who patiently read every draft and lovingly cheered me on from the start.